He'd have to trust her

Austin hated and loved the thought all at once. His heart contracted. He sighed heavily. Maxie was exquisite, lying next to him, in wild, naked abandon. Her smooth arms were poised over her head, her sweet lips parted slightly and her golden blond hair so silky to his touch.

He reached over her and under the bed, where he'd secreted the key. Very gently, he unlocked the cuffs and set her wrists free. Then he moved over her, and as if her mouth were a beacon in the dark, lonely night, he took it. Her lips were hot and wet, and held a hint of more pleasures to be revealed. He kissed her mouth roughly, opening her lips with his tongue only to be met by her eagerness and hunger.

Maxie acted on her own feelings of possession when she took his face between her hands to draw him closer, deeper.

He groaned, a dark sound full of craving.

For her.

She whimpered, an impatient song filled with need.

Of him.

Dear Reader,

How far would you go for your sister?

That's what my characters have to decide in *Hot on Her Tail*. Sexy bounty hunter Austin Taggart must collect on his latest bail jumper to give his gifted, artistic sister a head start on her career. Unfortunately, he has a weakness for damsels in distress and for this knight in shining armor, he's tortured between doing his duty or following his heart.

Francesca "Maxie" Maxwell also is in quite a tight situation— besides being handcuffed to her sexy captor. She must stay on the run until her name is cleared in an embezzlement scheme or she and her sister could lose their hip new nightclub, Firecrackers, along with their life savings.

I really enjoyed pairing this free-spirit heroine with my by-the-book hero and watching the sparks fly. Please let me know what you think. You can write to me at P.O. Box 1929, Centreville, VA 20122 or visit me at karenanders.com and drop me an e-mail.

Enjoy!

Karen Anders

P.S. Don't forget to check out tryblaze.com!

Books by Karen Anders

HARLEQUIN BLAZE
22—THE BARE FACTS

HOT ON HER TAIL

Karen Anders

TORONTO • NEW YORK • LONDON
AMSTERDAM • PARIS • SYDNEY • HAMBURG
STOCKHOLM • ATHENS • TOKYO • MILAN • MADRID
PRAGUE • WARSAW • BUDAPEST • AUCKLAND

To my supportive, loving sister Donna.
I would go on the run for you
or should I say, Kar-run!
Thanks for always being there!

ISBN 0-373-79047-3

HOT ON HER TAIL

Copyright © 2002 by Karen Alarie.

This edition published by arrangement with Harlequin Books S.A.

Visit us at www.eHarlequin.com

Printed in U.S.A.

1

―――――

AUSTIN TAGGART WAS A MAN who knew trouble when he saw it.

The picture of the woman burned his hands, made his breathing quicken and his hormones hop like Mexican jumping beans. Her skin was that pale porcelain that seemed to glow from some kind of inner light. Even in a photograph, her eyes were a deep mesmerizing blue and seemed to suck at his soul with the power of a tornado.

"Ah, damn, Manny." Austin sent the file flying across the desk, wiping his hands on his jeans as if in danger of catching a disease from the photograph. "Is this all you have?"

Manny Santana, Austin's source of income and one of Sedona's few bail bondsmen, looked up at Austin, his eyes narrowing. "How many years have you been doing this job?"

"Three. What does that have to do with anything?"

"In all the three years that you've been in this job, you aren't going to find an easier skip for such a huge payoff."

"She doesn't look easy to me."

"What are you talking about, *amigo?* I saved Francesca Maxwell for you. The bank where she worked is offering a reward of ten percent if the money she embezzled is recovered. I'm telling you. This is a cakewalk."

"She's trouble."

"How can she be trouble?" Manny looked down at the file and laughed. "Francesca Maxwell's never been arrested before, weighs all of a hundred and fifteen pounds soaking wet, and looks like an angel."

"I can tell. She's no cakewalk." A woman who looked this good was big trouble in Austin's book. Besides, she was blond. Just the thought of touching that spiky, silky-looking, windblown hair made his fingers tingle. She was nicely curved, with huge innocent-looking baby blues that could make the devil himself ask God for a favor. He wondered what her voice sounded like. Husky, he guessed. He felt a stirring of panic deep in his gut. No way was he going after this woman. In any way.

Manny looked perplexed and then his face cleared as if a lightbulb had gone off in his head. "Is this the blond thing, *amigo?* Damn you with your Indian hocus-pocus spiritualism. Just because it happened to you once doesn't mean you'll do it again. It's easy money."

"Don't scoff. My gut instinct has never let me down. Shelly? You remember her?" Yeah, look at what had happened with Shelly. He'd been all moon-eyed about the blonde and she had kicked him really hard in his pride. It still smarted. She played him for a fool and he fell for it hook, line and sinker. He leaned on the desk and looked Manny straight in the eye. Shelly had hurt him deeper than any woman he'd ever known, because he thought he had loved her. "Count me out."

"Look. I'm telling you. This is easy money." Manny picked up the photo and held it out to him. "She's a little Pollyanna who'll probably faint from your big, bad attitude."

Austin felt his gut tighten and a sixth sense whisper across his skin, raising the hair on the back of his neck. Austin hardened his features and decided that his gut pulled rank over Manny. He wasn't going anywhere near the woman.

"How much did she embezzle?"

"A cool million."

"A million?"

"That's right."

"How did she get caught?"

"I think somebody turned her in. But hey, I don't ask questions. When someone skips out on me and I stand to lose greenbacks, I get cranky."

"You've got the wrong guy, Manny."

"Austin, go pick her up, bring her back and collect your paycheck. With your tracking skills, it shouldn't take you more than a day or two," he said firmly, holding out the file.

Austin threw up his hands as if to protect his face. He stepped back from the desk. "No way, man. Call me if you need help apprehending a mad dog-killer or an international terrorist. I'd rather take them over this hell's angel.''

''You're a sissy. Come on, Renegade.''

Austin broke the rules when it suited him. But there was one rule he never broke. He always listened to his gut instincts, hocus-pocus or not.

Austin stepped back, his throat closing as if the air in Manny's little office was beginning to seep away. The look on Manny's face was comical. It was clear he thought Austin had lost his mind, but Austin knew better.

He got a glimpse of the photo as Manny sorted through the file. A breeze from the oscillating fan made the photo jump and, as it flattened, it looked as if she was winking at him. He backed up another pace. ''I'm telling you, Manny. My gut instincts say she's trouble. I'm outta here.''

Turning on his heel, he tried to quell the panic in his gut. He pulled open the door and stepped into the hot, dry heat of an Arizona summer, grateful to be out of the confines of Manny's office. This part of town wouldn't be showcased in any tourist brochure, but, then, it wasn't run-down either. Without being a hotbed of crime and vice, Sedona had enough law-breakers to make him a good living.

He dug in his jeans pocket for the keys to his sleek, black Mustang and unlocked the door. As cocky as if he had cheated death, he took a deep, cleansing breath. Whistling a merry tune, he settled himself in the seat. Starting the car, he turned the air on full blast, trying to breathe around the dense heat in the enclosed car. Immediately he saw that the "check oil" warning light was on. He made a call to his mechanic and got an appointment for the man to look at it by the end of the day.

The car had been his father's and Austin took care of it like it was his child. Besides a worn out picture, it was the only legacy he had left of a father he had loved deeply and lost at too young an age.

He tried to ignore the tightness in his chest while he toyed with the idea of stopping at Cactus Pete's for a long pull on a cold beer, but changed his mind. His grandmother had to be at the doctor's for her checkup at one-thirty and he didn't have the time. He wouldn't dream of keeping his ninety-year-old grandmother waiting or let his mother down. His stepfather had done that enough to last her a lifetime.

The trip from Sedona to the outskirts of town took no more than twenty minutes. Although he'd grown up here, he never could get over the awe of the spectacular scenery. In the distance, the startling formations of deep-red rock structures hunched against an almost perpetual blue sky. He loved the wide-open spaces, the evidence that Mother Nature was a force to be reckoned with. Part of his heritage, he guessed.

He pulled into the driveway of a four bedroom, two-story home with a detached guest house where he lived separate from the women in his family. With the help of his mother, who worked as a social worker, he supported his grandmother and sister. He was proud of the house he and his mother had been able to buy with their combined income. Jessica, his sister, was away at art school, honing her considerable talent. She was due back in a few days after her finals were finished.

He turned the engine off and sat in his car for a few moments, already feeling the effects of the heat waiting for him with a smothering embrace outside the car. Sweat trickled between his shoulder blades and soaked into his black muscle T-shirt. The woman's face was imprinted on his retinas and he couldn't banish her image. He was sure he'd made the right choice. He was already obsessed with a photo. How would he react to the real thing?

His cell phone rang as he was making his way up the walk. He pulled it off his belt and answered.

''Taggart.''

''You sound like a mean, tough bounty hunter, big brother.''

Austin smiled. ''Hey, shouldn't you be studying for finals, brat?''

''I took a break because I was so excited I had to call you. My watercolor instructor thinks I have amazing talent.''

''You do.''

''Thanks, Austin. Anyway, he's encouraged me to study with him this summer in a handpicked class in France. This is a chance of a lifetime.''

''That's great, Jessica.''

There's only one drawback.'' Her voice dropped an octave and an unsettling sense of dread moved through him.

''What's that?''

"The cost."

He braced himself and asked, "How much?" When Jessica told him the amount, his stomach lurched.

"It's too much, isn't it?"

Austin couldn't stand the sadness in her voice. His sister deserved this chance to make it. A chance he had never had. He'd been twenty-three the first time he'd seen his fifteen-year-old sister. Dirty, hanging onto his mother's arm as if she was the only safe haven in the world. He had promised himself he would give her everything he possibly could. If this meant a little self-sacrifice on his part, then so be it. Now, he would give her Paris, because she deserved it.

There was only one way he could get that kind of money. "When do you need it?"

"Next week. I know it's short notice, and I normally wouldn't ask, but this could lead to really big things, Austin. Maybe my own show someday."

He could hear the hope in his sister's voice and his heart sank. Going after that irresistible, troublesome skip went against every fiber of his being. The thought of getting near the woman made him nervous as hell, but Austin knew he would breach his one golden rule for Jessica. "Consider it a done deal. Call me later with the details on where to send the cash."

"Thanks, Austin. You're the best."

He released his breath and entered the house as he was dialing the phone.

"Sedona's Bail Bonds," Manny answered.

"Did you give that skip away yet?"

"No. You changed your mind?"

"Yeah. I'll be by to pick up the paperwork."

He walked into the kitchen, where his grandmother was sitting at the table, piecing together a puzzle.

"Are you ready to go, Grandmother?"

"Come sit with me for a moment, Austin."

Austin sat down at the table. "What is it?"

She put her hand on his forearm and he could feel the heat of her wisdom seep into him. His grandmother had been a medicine woman, revered by her tribe, but after his full-blooded Apache father had died, his mother had married a white man and they had left his grandmother behind at the reservation.

It had only been a year ago when his grandmother had gotten too old to practice the ways. He had brought her to live with them.

In the time of old, medicine women were given the responsibility of making the warriors' shields, for it was believed she had special powers that would give the war shields added protection for those who carried them. He covered his grandmother's hand, bending down to hear what she had to say. "I dreamed that you were chasing the sun."

"Is there danger in this, Grandmother?"

"Yes, of a kind, but one you will battle and overcome because you have the soul of a great warrior." She turned away and picked up a handwoven bag. She rummaged around inside and pulled an article out of the bag, her wrinkled fist closing around it.

"I will always try to make you proud of my spirit, Grandmother."

"One caution."

"Yes?"

The hand she returned to his forearm tightened. She brought her other hand around and opened it. In her palm sat a miniature warrior's shield. She took his hand and pressed the small object into his palm. "You cannot catch the sun without getting burned."

IT WAS LATER that afternoon, after he'd taken his grandmother home and then stopped by Manny's to pick up the paperwork that he paid a visit to Dorrie and Francesca Maxwell's soon-to-be opened club, Firecrackers.

The place was upscale and trendy, the sign a combination of lettering and starbursts of color.

When he entered, he passed a large mirrored wall and called out. "Hello. Anyone here?" The empty marble and glass room echoed his voice.

"Yes. Can I help you?" A woman called out as she popped up from behind the gleaming mahogany bar, a glass in her hand. He glimpsed honey blond hair, a blue tank top tucked into a pair of black slacks, and a nice little figure. Not the angel in question, but a cherub.

"Hi. I'm Austin Taggart from the Arizona Liquor Licensing Bureau."

She straightened and immediately came from behind the bar. "Is there a problem with Maxie's application for a license?'' Even though she tried to hide it, her voice quavered.

''Maxie?''

''Sorry. That's Francesca's nickname.''

''I see. I have a few questions that I need to ask her. I was hoping to get this cleared up because I'm sure you'd like to open on time.''

''Could I help you with that? I'm her sister Dorrie and also her partner.''

''I'm sorry, but I need the information from the person who applied for the license. Would it be possible for me to talk to your sister?'' The woman did a good job hiding her anxiety, but Austin was very observant and he caught the flash of alarm in her eyes.

''Well, she's not exactly reachable at this time. Could I take your number?''

''We take these matters very seriously, Ms. Maxwell.'' He wrote his cell phone number on a pad of paper sitting on the bar.

Suddenly, there was the sound of shattering glass in the back and Dorrie Maxwell closed her eyes in one of the flinching, cringing ways that told him she'd had a rough few days. Through clenched teeth, she said, ''I'm sure that you do. Could you please excuse me for just a moment?''

She turned and made her way to the back where deliveries were made. He could hear her yelling.

As soon as she was gone, Austin was behind the bar going through anything he could find. He spied a woman's purse and looked over his shoulder. Dorrie was still haranguing the delivery guy. He opened the bag and discovered that she must have just picked up her mail from their post office box. He riffled through bills and junk mail until he came to a postcard.

Bingo.

When Dorrie came back in, he wished her well with the new club and exited out the door. Walking around to the rear entrance, he found the red-faced deliveryman and slipped him a hundred dollars. It was double what he had promised, but hell, the guy had taken an awful lot of abuse.

IT WAS A TYPICAL raucous Saturday night for the notorious motorcycle hangout, Lucky Star. By midnight, Francesca ''Maxie'' Maxwell's scanty barmaid outfit was beer-stained and her nerves were frayed from three hours of sidestepping slaps and tickles. She set down a mug of white-foamed beer in front of a man who couldn't stop chuckling to himself, made a mental note that it was last call for him, at least, and glanced over at the bartender, Star Dupree. Maybe Star would let Maxie call a taxi for this fella. He was a regular, and Star, the owner and former motorcycle mama, took good care of her regulars. But Star wasn't paying attention as she dispensed both drinks and wisdom behind the bar. She was a formidable woman with dramatic fiery red hair and stars tattooed all over the cleavage of her large bosoms. She slapped a patron on the arm, letting out the loud, honking laugh that she was famous for.

Maxie had been lucky when she happened upon Mesa Roja, a sleepy, little New Mexico town just about seven-hundred miles from Sedona. It was far enough away, yet close enough to suit her if she needed to get back to Sedona in a hurry.

A jukebox was playing country music. Men were milling about the bar and playing pool, occupying all six pool tables. In the corner behind the pool tables, Maxie caught the thunking sound of darts as patrons attempted to hit the bull's-eye.

A huge man with a black handlebar mustache called out from a nearby table. "Come on, Maxie, why don't you sit a spell on my lap."

The other men at the table all laughed.

"And I sure could use a sit-down, but Handlebar, Star don't pay me for sitting, sugar. Now you wouldn't want me to lose my job, would you?"

She bent down and pinched his cheek, giving him a brilliant smile. "Besides. I don't think it's me you're sweet on," she whispered softly, glancing at Star as she tended bar.

Handlebar flushed and followed her gaze. He smiled sheepishly.

As she turned back toward the bar, exasperation filled her chest. Who would have thought she'd have a good time in such a place? Firecrackers, the night-club her sister was busy getting ready to open, was a much more sophisticated place, that was true. But these people were down-to-earth and, most of them, although they looked tough, had hearts of gold.

With thoughts of Firecrackers came the guilt-ridden thoughts of her sister and that she was alone, doing all the work. In the past, Maxie had taken it for granted that her sister would always be there to help her out. After all, she had taken care of Maxie since she'd been sixteen. Unable to handle the constant harping of her mother and the disapproval of her father, Maxie had run away from home. Dorrie hadn't complained once. Not once. Her sweet sister wasn't complaining now either. She'd shouldered the responsibility, insisting that Maxie was innocent of all embezzlement charges, and forged along with plans to open the club.

She rubbed at her temples, the noise in the bar giving her a headache. As a bank manager, a stuffy job she'd hated, she wasn't used to all this noise. She put her hands on the bar and, for just a moment, leaned on it to rest. Her feet were throbbing; and her legs were on fire, and she wondered why any woman in her right mind would do such a job on a regular basis. Yet, she loved it.

The heat blast from the door opening engulfed her like a scorching blanket, caressing her from neck to toes. She turned, instinctively alert.

The source of that heat stood in the open door looking around as if he owned the place. All the air whooshed out of her lungs; her insides went liquid and her knees literally buckled. It'd been a long time since a man had dumbfounded Maxie.

But this was no ordinary man.

A fizzle of warning stirred in her stomach. This man was her physical type from the top of his dark head to the tips of his boots. He looked full-blooded Apache, judging by his thick hair and high, chiseled cheekbones. His stunning golden brown eyes traveled her body in an admiring, languorous slide. Stark white teeth flashed against the dimness of the bar. Oh baby, what a mouth, full gorgeous lips made for kissing.

He wore a pair of tight jeans that fit snug across his groin. A black T-shirt with the slogan *Attitude? What Attitude?* stretched across his wide, well-muscled chest. His straight hair was as black as a raven's wing and reached to touch the cotton neck of the shirt.

She knew she was staring with her mouth wide open. Heel, girl. She was already knee-deep in trouble and the last thing she needed in her life right now was this type of heartbreaker.

Although, one night with this man might be worth a little heartache. He was every woman's dream and every father's nightmare.

He took an empty table near the door, one that afforded him a good view of the bar but protected his back. Another frisson of warning fizzled in Maxie's stomach. Who was this guy? A stranger, that was for sure, and strangers in this small town made her nervous.

It had been almost a month since she'd skipped bail to save the club and no one had come after her. Yet he was obviously cagey, protecting his back. Could he be here for her?

She took a deep breath, knowing that if he was looking for someone, bolting right now wouldn't be smart.

She walked up to the table and flashed him a smile.

He looked up at her, his eyes suddenly sliding out of focus.

"What can I get you, handsome?"

He didn't answer her right away, but continued staring at her as if he knew her.

His intense gaze made her even more nervous. Although he was a little too wild looking for a cop, he had cop eyes. Intelligent and guarded. "Mister?"

He blinked a couple of times and finally answered. "Beer." His voice was a low, sexy purr that made the hair on her arms stand up. She swallowed hard.

"What kind?"

"Whatever you have on tap."

She left the table feeling as if his eyes were burning a hole in her back. She went to the bar. "Hi Star, can you give me a beer?"

The woman smiled, and poured one from the tap. "Sure is hopping tonight, honey."

"It sure is. I'm going to have bruises from my ass all the way to my elbows."

Star laughed. "You watch your backside, honey. Keep them in line."

Maxie winked and picked up the man's drink. "Handlebar sure looks good tonight, huh Star? That's a fine figure of a man."

Star looked over at the tall, hard-muscled biker and flushed. "Why would I be interested in him, honey?"

"Oh, I don't know, maybe because you can't keep your eyes off him."

Star raised a brow. "Do I pay you for matchmaking or serving?"

Maxie laughed and turned away from her boss. As she was passing the jukebox, a patron was kicking it. "Spider! Stop that right now." Named for the huge tattoo he had of a spider on his back, he was a tall and lanky man with a shock of dyed white hair. She gave him a kick in the pants as she sidled by.

"It took my money!"

"Kicking it isn't going to help," she scolded.

"Hey, you kicked me," he said, looking indignant.

"That, on the other hand, will help." She flashed him a smile, aware that the stranger watched her every move. It made her skin tingle and her stomach do flip-flops. She pulled a quarter out of her apron pocket and flipped it to Spider. "Stop being a cheapskate."

She set the beer down on the man's table, but just as she turned away, he touched her arm. Startled by the heated contact of his hard, callused hand, Maxie turned back.

"Excuse me, but I'm trying to locate someone." His brown eyes, burning from within by an unholy flame, bore into hers as if he could see all the way to her soul. She shivered. She wouldn't want to be the one he was looking for...or maybe she would.

This close to him, she could smell his spicy scent, one that was wholly male. It made her head reel. The laughter and din of the bar receded.

He let go of her as if he'd been burned and she stepped back. "Sure, mister..." Out of the corner of her eye, she saw Frank try to sneak by her. "Please excuse me for a moment." She abandoned the stranger and stepped in Frank's path, blocking him from entering the bar.

Frank had just given her a good way to get the hell out of Dodge. The stranger made her nervous, but she wasn't sure if it was because he made her insides go haywire or because he exuded a dangerous, lethal quality. He could very well be looking for her.

"Frank. Isn't it payday today?"

"Ah Maxie. I just want one." He brushed past her and headed for the bar.

"Frank. You know you wouldn't stop at one." Maxie sidled around him, which also put her closer to the bar and the back door. "Now you go straight to the store and buy your babies some food. Then you give Tami the rest of that money."

"One to wet my whistle?" he pleaded.

Maxie jammed her hands on her hips and rolled her eyes. "Frank Duncan, I will personally buy a beer for you, if you go and take care of your family first."

"All right! You win, but I'm coming back for that beer!"

"You do that, Frank." Maxie knew that once he got home to his wife, he wouldn't be coming anywhere near this bar.

The stranger was much too alert. His brown eyes didn't move from her and Maxie knew that she'd better bolt now while she had the chance.

She slipped between two tables, but one man grabbed her arm and halted her.

"Maxie, I want another whiskey."

"Okay, Snake. Give me a minute." She hazarded

a glance at the stranger. His eyes were still on her. Trying to quell a burst of panic, she gave Snake a winning smile and he let her go.

A crash and the sound of breaking glass caught Maxie's attention. Handlebar was standing, well more like swaying, holding a piece of broken glass in his hand.

He was threatening Spider with it.

Maxie looked at the back door longingly, then at the stranger. She sighed. This would be a perfect time to get out of here—while there was this ready-made disruption. But Star had been good to her and she didn't want anything to happen to her establishment or her patrons.

She knew she could soothe Handlebar. He liked and trusted her, but it was her skin she should worry about. Then she made the mistake of looking in Star's direction. The worried expression on her face made up Maxie's mind. She wouldn't be able to forgive herself if something happened to the tenderhearted biker because she had turned her back.

Maxie sighed again and moved towards Handlebar. "Handlebar, you know you don't want to hurt Spider. He's your best drinking buddy. Besides, think of the mess I'd have to clean up."

He looked at her blearily. "He played that damn sad song. I told him not to, but he did it anyway."

"Give me the piece of glass, honey, before someone gets hurt."

A man at the table shouted. "Are you going to

kowtow to some piece of ass, Handlebar? Cut the bastard.''

''Handlebar, don't listen to him,'' Maxie cajoled. ''Listen to me. I know what's best for you, sugar.'' Handlebar stepped toward her, starting to relinquish the jagged bit of beer bottle.

Spider rose. ''You gonna cut me, Handlebar, well come on then. Go ahead.''

''What the hell do you think you're doing?''

Suddenly the stranger was there, stepping in front of her, blocking her view of the two circling men. Before Maxie could tell him to get out of her way, Handlebar lunged at Spider. Spider jumped backward and hit the stranger a solid blow. He, in turn, staggered into Maxie, who tried to get out of the way. But she was too late. She stumbled, her back coming up against a wall of muscle. A patron in the bar too drunk to stop his lecherous, impulsive behavior decided it was okay to grab her ass. Pure reaction caused Maxie to screech and turn around swinging. She connected solidly against his jaw. The man let out a bellow and instinctively swung at her.

But Maxie ducked, and the full force of the punch connected solidly with the stranger's jaw. He flew into a group of bikers at a pool table. And, like a domino effect, the men toppled. All of them came up swinging.

Someone hurled a chair, and Maxie knew there was no way she was going to be able to get out of the way in time. But miraculously, the stranger was there, breaking the full force of the chair's impact against his big body. He grunted in pain, but immediately turned toward her. Maxie wanted to run, but her feet seemed rooted to the floor by the man's intense hawk-like gaze. Taking hold of her upper arm, he dragged her toward the exit, but stopped when a group of men, just coming into the bar, joined in.

He swore vehemently under his breath. "Damn fool woman."

"Hey," Maxie protested as he pushed her against the wall near the bar and stood in front of her. How had this happened? She'd been trying to prevent chaos and she'd been the one to start it. If that stupid stranger had minded his own business, none of this would have happened. She'd be through the back door, grabbing up her belongings and hightailing it out of town.

The bar had turned into a melee of men pummeling each other. Bodies were flying everywhere, over the bar, smashing against tables, crashing into walls. Many tried to get past the big stranger's guard, but every time he was assaulted, he was the victor.

Over the din, she could hear the blare of approaching sirens. A few minutes later, deputies came barreling through the door. They broke up the fight and methodically began handcuffing men.

When a deputy walked over to the stranger, Maxie shoved her way out. She pushed on the stranger's big, muscled chest. "This is your fault. If you hadn't gotten in my way, this would never have happened."

"Wait a minute," he started to protest, his eyebrows snapping into a frown over those amazing eyes. Just the color of honey they were.

The deputy grabbed the stranger's arm and Maxie threw her hands up in the air. "Charlie. What are you doing? Can't you see I'm having a conversation here?"

"Sorry, ma'am. The sheriff says everyone goes." Just then Maxie spotted Sheriff Clem Stubbins standing in the doorway. She strode over to him. "Clem, that man over there started it." Maxie pointed at the stranger.

"Well, Miss Maxie, you sure about that?" the sheriff asked. He tipped his hat back and regarded her with sharp blue eyes.

Sheepishly Maxie said, "Well, he was partly to blame." She tried to sidle past him to go out the front door, but he grabbed a hold of her arm.

Clem's eyebrows lifted. "Let me guess. You were also partly to blame." His eyes twinkled.

"I reacted. It wasn't entirely my fault."

The sheriff smiled. "It never is, Maxie. Can you tell me exactly what happened?"

"I didn't actually see everything. I was busy covering my butt."

"What?"

"This big oaf put his hands on my...posterior and well, I reacted. I slugged him. One thing led to another..."

"Him?" The sheriff indicated the stranger.

"No not him. Some other oaf."

"Round everyone up, Charlie. We'll get this straightened out down at the jail."

"But, Clem…"

"Now, now, Maxie. Don't get your rope in a knot. We'll settle everything down at the jail. I'm getting too old for this," he muttered. "Retirement is looking better and better every day."

"Sheriff, could I have a word with you?" The stranger had walked over while Maxie was trying to give her side of the story. She was hoping the sheriff was going to let her go and haul the stranger off to jail. Just in case she needed a head start.

"What is it?" he said impatiently.

The man pulled out two pieces of paper and handed them to the sheriff.

Clem looked at the stranger, then at Maxie and sighed. "Can I see some ID?"

The stranger pulled out his wallet and flipped it open with a snap of his wrist. Maxie felt her stomach turn over. "Austin Taggart. They call you Renegade."

"That's right."

"I've heard of you. I'm going to caution you, boy. If I find out you haven't treated her with the utmost respect, I'll find you."

The stranger bristled, those amazing eyes turning dangerous, and Maxie could see that he wanted to tell the sheriff to go to hell, but he didn't.

The sheriff handed the paper back to Austin and then turned to give her a sad look. "It all seems in order, but listen Renegade, give me a good reason not to haul you to jail.''

''You could tie me up for a couple of hours, but it wouldn't change anything. Besides, all I did was protect blondie here from getting hurt.''

The sheriff addressed her. ''Is that true, Maxie?''

''Yes,'' she said reluctantly. ''It's true.''

The sheriff eyed Austin, deliberating. ''You're free to go.''

The sheriff walked away and Maxie was getting a real bad feeling about this.

''So who were you looking for, Mr. Taggart?''

He reached for her and captured her hand. The metal of the handcuff made a snicking sound as it latched around her wrist.

That soft husky voice made her insides go haywire at the same time it sent goose bumps of dread across her skin.

''Why, I'm looking for you, Ms. Maxwell.''

2

AUSTIN HAD BEEN A FOOL to take this job. Close up she was more beautiful and more innocent-looking than she'd been in the photograph. She came up to the middle of his chest, smaller than he'd envisioned, delicate like a pixie. Her features were even more compelling than in the photo, richer and so stunning it was hard for him to keep his mind on what he had to do. Her skin was soft to his touch, and warm, sending detonations of sensation down his arms. Her hair was honey blond and spiked around her head and face as if she'd just rolled out of some guy's bed. He clamped down on his damned inconvenient hormones and took hold of her other wrist. She pulled it out of his grasp and backed up.

"It's all a mistake."

The sound of her voice affected him way too much with its warm, deep sound. "In what way?" he asked in a purely uninterested voice.

"I didn't steal the money. I was framed." She struggled against his grip on her. Austin increased the pressure, aware that any more would probably bruise her, and he didn't want to hurt her or mar her lovely skin.

"I'm not going to argue with you about whether or not you're guilty. I'm here to take you back to Sedona and pick up my paycheck." He reached for her other wrist again but she jerked back, putting distance between them. The distance was good, but he wished she would stop struggling so that he could snap the other cuff on her. He wanted to take his hands off her. He didn't like the sensations that were pouring through him from the innocent contact of his hand around her wrist.

"That's exactly my dilemma. I can't go back just now. I need to stall for just a few more days."

He easily dragged her forward and thrust his face close to hers, having to bend down to do it. If reasoning wasn't going to work, he'd have to get mean. He hated to get mean, especially with such a small, delicate woman. "This is not a debate, blondie."

"Couldn't you just listen for a minute and stop calling me 'blondie'? My name is Maxie."

Did she think he'd been born yesterday? It clarified in his mind that she might be right out of a man's hot, sweaty fantasy, but she sure wasn't the sharpest knife in the drawer. Did she seriously believe she could talk him out of taking her back?

"No. It's not in my job description," he said tersely. "Don't make this hard on yourself."

"I have a guy working for me. As soon as Jake Utah clears my name, all this embezzlement business will be straightened out. I assure you."

"Blondie, jumping bail makes you my business. You see these pieces of paper?" He pulled them out of his back pocket and held them up for her. "They say you're mine."

Her eyes widened and he recognized the panic he saw building there. She was going to bolt. "Don't do it, blondie. I'm the best there is. If you *could* get away, you wouldn't get far." He grabbed her other wrist as she sidled backward.

Then out of nowhere, the Amazonian woman bartender with dark flaming red hair grabbed his arm. "Leave her alone, you big bully."

Her knee jerked into his crotch with the force of a battering ram. Austin grunted as white-hot agony set his groin on fire and doubled him over. With a groan, he slipped to his knees.

"Run, honey. Run!"

He glimpsed the blond nymph as she looked at the six-foot bartender, indecision in her lovely face. Blondie stared down at him with sympathy and apology in her deep blue eyes. Then she was opening the front door, the handcuffs clanging against the wood.

He glanced at the sheriff, who made no attempt to go after Maxie. That was the way the wind was blowing, huh? This whole town was going to protect her?

Austin couldn't breathe around the pain. He took shallow breaths, and a red, misty haze settled over his eyes. Damn, but that *hurt*.

He reached out and latched onto a chair and dragged himself to his feet. Ignoring the nausea that churned at the back of his throat, he took a step. Cold sweat broke out on his forehead, but he forced himself to relax and let the pain flow out of him. He'd had good practice at it. He made it to the door and jerked it open.

Stepping out into the moonlit parking lot, he looked around. Damn. That had never happened to him before. Bested by a middle-aged woman with star tattoos. Of course, she was at least six feet tall with serious muscles.

He always got his man. Right. *Man* was the important word. He knew this job was going to be trouble when he'd seen the skip's sweet, sincere face. Telling himself, *I told you so* didn't help in the least. He'd walk away right now if he didn't need the money, but he couldn't let his sister down. He'd made her a promise. And since he'd gone to the reservation and saved her from a life of poverty, he could never renege on that promise. Not ever.

He hit the side of the building in frustration. Now where had his little skipper skipped to?

MAXIE DIDN'T HAVE to go far, since Star had included room and board along with her wage. Her room was behind the bar and Maxie raced around the small area, stuffing as many of her things as she could into the small bag she'd taken for her jaunt.

Ha! The magnitude of her problem was just becoming clear to her. The bail bondsman had sent a bounty hunter after her, one who was tenacious and, as he said, good at his job. A man shot through with western steel. She was in deep, deep trouble.

Star came into the room. "Here, honey." She

thrust money into Maxie's hand, along with keys to her hog.

Maxie's eyes suddenly burned. "Star, I can't take your ride." Maxie tried to thrust the keys back, but Star held up her palms.

"I don't know what kind of trouble you're in, but I know some good lawyers. I'll get you one. You call me when you get somewhere safe."

Tears pricked the back of Maxie's eyes at Star's generosity and fullness of heart. Who would have guessed a former motorcycle mama would care? "I can tell you that it's all a misunderstanding."

Star cupped her cheek. "I know that. You've been in this town just shy of a month and you're a favorite. Patrons come to my bar just to be near your sweet smile."

Maxie's hand tightened around the money and the key. "Thanks." She put both in her fanny pack and turned to reach for her backpack, feeling queasy when the handcuffs swung forward.

"Star, what about the handcuffs?" Maxie looked down at them with dread, and a sick sensation made her throat close.

"No problem, honey. You go see my friend Seymour and he'll get the cuffs off." Star picked up a pad of paper sitting on the nightstand and scribbled a name and address.

Maxie accepted the slip of paper, again stuffing it into her fanny pack. "Star, you could get into a lot of trouble for aiding and abetting a fugitive."

"Honey, you ain't no fugitive—you're my friend.

The law can go to hell." Star looked out the window. "You stay here while I lock up the bar and until I tell you it's all clear."

Star left the room and Maxie went to the bed and pushed the small bag out of the way. She sat down, leaning her back against the wall. Closing her eyes, she took a deep breath and let it out.

A few weeks ago, she'd been a respected bank manager who had just resigned her position to open up a long held dream—Firecrackers. Now, she was a fugitive from justice wanted for embezzlement from the First Security Bank in Sedona. She had no idea where the money, she was supposed to have taken, had gone. They had grilled her about that money for hours, but she couldn't tell them because she didn't know.

She'd hated that job and it had been a chore to stick it out the five years she'd worked there, but the pittance in her bank account was hers. She was baffled to find her password and her authority abused. Someone had taken from numerous personal accounts of the bank's patrons to the tune of one million dollars.

Thank God for Jake. He had assured Maxie that he would help her out by looking through all the computer generated information available to try to find out who had framed her. Unfortunately, that took a lot of time and she would have to stall until he came through with the name of the perpetrator. The authorities had stopped looking—they had her.

She'd wait until Star said it was safe and then she'd find herself another small town in New Mexico and stay one step ahead of that hard-as-nails bounty hunter.

Maxie sat anxiously on the bed waiting for Star to come back. She glanced at the clock and saw that it was getting close to two in the morning.

Maxie jumped when Star came back into the room. "It's all clear, honey."

"You haven't seen him?"

"No, I think he's gone."

"Is he still in town?"

"No way to tell. We don't have time to make sure, but I haven't seen his Mustang. That car isn't easy to miss." Star talked in hushed tones as if the bounty hunter were just outside the window listening. Maxie shivered at the thought.

Maxie grabbed her bag, walked to the door and peered out. Even with the heat of the desert, Maxie felt a chill travel over her skin.

"You're certain he's nowhere around here?"

"Can't say for sure, but it looks clear. You can't wait much longer. Go now, honey. Call me when you can."

Maxie hugged Star hard. "I will. Thanks for everything."

The hair on Maxie's neck lifted as she stepped out into the moonlit night. She looked up at the sky dotted with a thousand stars. It was so beautiful in the desert—too bad she didn't have the time to enjoy it. She walked to the side of the bar and peered around the corner. The parking lot was empty, the bar closed for the night because all Star's patrons were in the local jail. Star's motorcycle sat half in and half out of the shadow of the bar's overhang.

Maxie shivered, but there was no one there. Her fingers trembled as she groped for the keys to the bike, but she couldn't seem to get her hands on them. She'd wait until she was in the light and find them. She couldn't stand here on the verge of a nervous breakdown all night. Gathering her courage, she strode forward. Reaching the bike, she straddled the seat and reached inside the fanny pack. The security light from the bar fell on the interior of the fanny pack and illuminated the keys. Just as she spied them, a dark, deep, raspy voice curled around her, seeping into her bones.

"Miss me?"

Her body tightened like a coiled spring, her heart jumping into her throat. He pulled her off the bike and grabbed her wrists. With quick efficiency, he locked the loose handcuff tight to her free wrist.

Maxie looked up at him as he loomed over her. He peered down at her as the night wind lifted his sleek black hair. There was nothing welcoming or gentle in his expression. His unrelenting stare speared her, slashing like steel, cutting, seeing what ran beneath skin and masqueraded as control. There was an unnerving quality in his eyes as he looked at her. Awe? Hunger? She couldn't be sure it wasn't merely the play of light and shadow. When she tried a tentative smile to put him off guard, the steady gaze of his dark eyes hardened.

This man had seen some hard living. And she had

no doubt that he was good at what he did. He fit the image of a bounty hunter with his soaring black eyebrows, piercing eyes, a nose that angled slightly at the bridge, cutting through the breadth of his wide, blunt cheekbones, followed by a sensuous mouth that curved slowly as he watched her. Dark skinned, a heritage of his Native American ancestors. Apache, she thought, the evidence in his sharp, angled, breath stealing face.

"Don't fight me. Don't run from me. It won't do you any good and it ticks me off."

He dragged her up against him and she could feel the hard heat of his chest, smell the intoxicating male scent as wave after wave of pleasure ignited inside her.

"I don't want you ticked off, right?" she challenged without flinching or looking away from him.

His predatory smile flashed in the night. "No."

"I guess they don't call you Renegade for nothing."

"A fearless pixie with sarcasm."

Maxie felt the unfamiliar sense of annoyance flash through her. She gave him a smug, dirty look. To him she was nothing but chattel and she resented the fact that he thought she was dumb.

"Darlin', don't look at me like that. You can't pass it off."

"Like what?" she asked, her anger rising.

"Like you can outsmart me."

"You can't be outsmarted?" She pushed at his chest with her manacled hands, a hard chest that made her hands want to open so she could explore his muscles.

"Not by you."

"Why is that?"

"Darlin', ditsy blondes don't have the sense God gave a turnip."

"Ditsy?" Maxie put her hands on her hips and gave him the dirtiest look she could muster.

"Is THAT LOOK supposed to scare me?" Austin said, thinking that she looked cute and adorable with her face scrunched up. Austin felt those damn hormones kicking up again. He deliberately stepped away from her. "You tried to stop a fight between two men who could squash you like a bug. One of them had a broken beer bottle. You could have bled to death. I'd call that pretty stupid." He could still see the scene. Those men could have hurt her really bad. He felt his protective instincts rise up along with the gut-wrenching fear.

"I would have gotten the bottle from him and stopped the bar fight if you hadn't stuck your arrogant nose into it," she sniffed.

"You're too ditsy to know how ditsy you are."

"You'll pay for that," she threatened.

"Sure, I will."

He grabbed the handcuffs by the chain and dragged her to the car, which he'd concealed off the road not far from the bar. When he got there, he pulled her forward against the hood, stepped behind her and kicked her feet apart.

And hesitated.

Do it man, he said to himself. He wasn't worried that she had a weapon, but it was common practice to shake each skip down to make sure.

Do it.

His hands went over her body so fast it couldn't even be called a frisk, more like a brisk.

"What the…heck was that?" were her muffled words as she turned around.

He stepped back. "I frisked you."

She laughed. "You call that a frisk?"

Sweat popped out on his forehead. He wasn't going to touch her no matter how much she goaded him.

She stepped close to him and he jumped back.

She smiled slow and catlike. "Do *I*, little ol' me, intimidate *you?*"

"No."

"No?" she mimicked. "Then frisk me like you're supposed to. I could be carrying a weapon," she challenged, pushing against his chest.

He snorted. "You couldn't possibly be carrying any weapons in those shorts."

She looked down at her attire. "It's the bar's uniform. I have to wear these to work."

His eyebrows lowered into a frown, angry because he would enjoy sending his hands over her body. "I don't get off manhandling women." He opened the passenger side door. "Watch your head," he advised, placing his hand on the top of her head to protect it as he guided her into the Mustang.

He walked around the car and got into the driver's

seat. Inserting the key into the ignition, he started the car.

"What does get you off?" Maxie asked.

His hand jerked and the unmistakable sound of a car being started while it was already running grated against his eardrums.

He winced at the sound. "I'm not falling for this, blondie."

"Call me Maxie. Falling for what?"

"Sexual overtures aren't going to get you off the hook. But if you're offering, I don't want any boo-hooing in the morning." He had no intention of following through with that threat. He wasn't going to get up close and personal with his bounty. It would be sheer stupidity.

"I'm not making sexual overtures, and I never regret great sex. I'm just curious."

"You know what they say about curiosity." Great sex? Damn. Was she crazy propositioning a male she didn't know anything about? She was under his complete control, yet she seemed fearless.

"Sure. It killed the cat, but I'm no cat."

He looked at her as if he didn't believe her, but he could see that she was dead serious. Her innocent eyes beckoned him. "You're curious about what gets me off?"

"Sure."

Scaring her seemed like a good idea. "Hot little pixies in short shorts asking me what gets me off."

"Oh."

He smiled, glad that he had finally quieted her down.

"What else?"

This woman didn't know when to quit. "I'm not having this discussion with you."

"Austin...may I call you Austin or should I call you 'Renegade'?"

"Silence would be your best choice."

"I bet you would like that. Then you wouldn't have to get to know me and realize that I didn't steal anything."

"Tell it to the judge." Austin wasn't going to get suckered into believing all that innocence that floated around her like an aura. He wasn't going to talk to her any more.

"But...I just need to stall."

"My job is to bring you in. End of story."

Maxie sat there for a moment and he breathed a sigh of relief that she was finally going to keep quiet. Her voice was more powerful in an enclosed place and did crazy things to his insides. But then she spoke again.

"We're not going to drive seven hundred miles straight. Are we?"

"No. As soon as I find a suitable place, I'll stop. I'm dead tired."

"You look it. Didn't get much sleep?"

He gave her a sidelong glance. "No. I was tracking you."

"How did you do that, by the way?"

"I went to your club." He ran his hand through

his hair. How did he get suckered into answering her when he'd just vowed he wasn't going to answer her?

"And?"

He let out a long-suffering sigh. "I posed as an employee from the liquor licensing bureau."

"You tricked Dorrie into telling you where I was?"

"Not exactly. I paid a delivery guy to cause a ruckus and distract your sister."

"Then you searched her personal belongings."

"That's right. Your sister had a postcard from you postmarked from Mesa Roja. After that I drove here, asked around. Everyone knew you, where you worked, told me real nice stories about you. Gotta love a small town."

She sighed and leaned her head back. "So you knew I lived in the room behind the bar. Why didn't you just knock on the door and apprehend me?"

"I didn't want to have another tussle with your employer. My balls still ache." He shifted in the seat. They did hurt with a dull throbbing, but it had nothing to do with being kneed in the groin. "I know how fugitives behave. I knew you'd run sooner or later, so I waited until your employer closed up."

"Why would the townspeople talk to you?"

"Told them I was your husband and that we'd had a spat. I said I'd make nice and fetch you home."

"I bet you're a good liar."

"I don't enjoy it, but it's part of the job."

She lapsed into silence and Austin was thankful. He concentrated on driving the almost barren stretch of NM 64 that ran alongside the Santa Fe Trail. He estimated that it should take them about an hour and a half to make Cimarron and then Taos by daybreak. He tried to keep his eyes from straying over to her mouth-watering legs bared all the way up to the top of her thigh. Those shorts were scandalous. He hoped she had something else to wear inside the beat up bag she was carrying. They went through Raton a blur of streetlights and closed shops. Shortly after that, his head nodded and he swerved suddenly. Maxie grabbed his arm.

"I think we'd better stop, now."

"I think you're right."

"We'll have to go back to Raton because there is nothing between Raton and Cimarron. I think you're too tired to make Cimarron. I saw a motel a few miles back," she said, removing her manacled hands from his arm.

It didn't take long for him to do a U-turn and head back the way they had come. In the distance, he could see a sign for the Sands Motel.

When he reached the entrance, Austin pulled over and shut off the engine. The one-level cinder-block motel didn't look like much from the outside, but if it had a bed and bathroom, he didn't care about the appearance. He pulled the key out of his pocket and unlocked one wrist, threaded the handcuff through the steering wheel and snapped it back on her wrist. "I'll be right back."

"I'll count the minutes."

He checked them in and got the key. Walking back

to the car, he pulled their belongings out and transferred them to their surprisingly large and well-cared-for room. Wood paneling darkened the walls and a double bed sat invitingly against curtained double-wide windows. He dropped the bags on the bed and went after the skip.

The moment they were in the room, Maxie held out her hands. "Could you take these off? I'd like to take a quick shower."

He snorted. "*Quick* and *female* are two incompatible words."

"I'm sure you have plenty of experience with women," she said with a raised brow.

"I should. I live with three of them."

Both eyebrows rose in surprise. "Three women?"

He smiled at the stunned look on her face. "My sister, my mother and my grandmother."

"Oh. How old is your sister?"

"Nineteen. She's finishing up her first year at Yale. She's majoring in art." Before he realized what he was doing, he reached back and pulled out his wallet. Flipping open the worn leather, he placed the wallet in her hands. "That's her high-school graduation picture. She graduated at the top of her class." His chest swelled with the pride he felt for her achievements. She looked so happy in her black cap and gown, a wide grin on her pretty face.

"What's her name?"

"Jessica."

"She's beautiful and I can tell you're really proud of her."

The soft look in Maxie's blue eyes made him shuffle his feet. There was nothing he enjoyed talking about more. Suddenly realizing that he had related something personal to a skip trace, he took the wallet back and snapped it closed, sliding it into his back jeans pocket. "Anyway, I know how long women take in the shower."

The skip eyed him, the soft look replaced with one of puzzlement. "Okay, have it your way. I'm going to take a long, hot shower and I'll need my hands."

He immediately, ruthlessly suppressed the image of her hot soapy hands traveling over her lush naked curves. He jammed his hand into the pocket of his suddenly tight jeans and produced the handcuff key.

"Just a minute." He walked to the bathroom and opened the door. There were no windows, just a tub and toilet in the small room.

He walked back to her and unlocked the cuffs. Maxie picked up the small, lightweight backpack and headed for the bathroom.

THE MOMENT SHE SHUT the door, she grabbed a towel off the rack. She pulled up on the shorts, tucking them in so that the hem didn't show. She slipped the round-necked shirt off her shoulders along with her bra straps. Then she wrapped the towel around her as tight as she could. She caught her eye in the mirror and hesitated. Guilt assaulted her. So the guy had a family, so he loved his sister and was proud of her. She was nothing to him but a paycheck and he could easily find another bounty. If Maxie didn't escape, she was looking at major time in jail because theft from a bank was a federal crime. She wasn't going to jail for a crime she didn't commit. She also couldn't bear the thought that they would lose Firecrackers. Without a liquor license, they couldn't open on time. Although Jake was on the job, he hadn't been able to turn up any information to help clear her name.

She stood there a moment, breathing deep, trying to get her heart to race. Then she let out a bloodcurdling scream.

"Maxie!" Austin banged on the door. She stepped to the door and threw it open with as much drama as she could muster.

"Austin!" she yelled, throwing herself at him, winding her arms around his neck as if she were never going to let go. She added the shaking because she thought it would give her story more credence.

"Maxie, what is it?"

She shuddered for the full effect.

"It's okay," he said softly, his hand coming up to cup the back of her head. Guilt assaulted her again, he was such a protective guy and here she was tricking him. But at this point, she had no choice. The feel of his fingers in her hair, against the sensitive skin of her scalp sent real shivers down her back.

The guy was built. His shoulders were heavily muscled, the feel of his hair like hot silk against her bare arms. She wished she had the time to explore this man because she had no doubt that she could get him into bed. She let her hand slip down his body to his belt.

When she had the cell phone in her hand she said, "There's a spider in the bath tub!"

Austin motioned for her to go to the tub and followed her into the bathroom. The small enclosure seemed to shrink with his presence. He eyed her towel, his gaze lingering on the swell of her breasts.

She stepped forward and placed her hand on his forearm. The heat of him was intoxicating, but that wasn't why she was doing this little song and dance. He looked deep into her eyes and stepped closer to her. "Austin, the spider."

"Spider?"

"In the tub."

He looked at the closed shower curtain and then at her, his eyes clearing and wariness surfacing. He moved closer to the tub and she took a step toward the door. As he reached for the shower curtain, she braced herself against the wall. Just as he bent over to peer into the tub, she shoved with her foot. He went flying forward into the tub.

She could hear his head hit with a dull thud and he cried out in pain, but she couldn't let it dissuade her.

Maxie turned, scooped up her bag and bolted out of the bathroom, slamming the door behind her. With a quick, panicky movement, she placed the chair sitting next to the bathroom under the handle. She threw the cell phone onto the bed and ripped off the towel, pulling up her bra straps and shirt, pulling down her hiked up shorts.

"Maxie. Open this goddamned door."

He was only doing his job and she respected that. But she couldn't let her sister down. This mess was all hers and the embezzlement charges endangered Firecrackers. She had to stay on the lam until that license came through or she could clear her name, but if not, her sister would, at least, be provided for.

"When I get out of here...open the door, now!"

The bonus of eluding the great Renegade made her smile. She had to protect her interests. Stalling this tough, streetwise bounty hunter wasn't going to be easy, but she wasn't just going docilely back to Sedona. She and Dorrie had their life savings tied up in Firecrackers. Dorrie was depending on her, and this time she wasn't going to let her sister down. She bit her lip. If only Jake could find out who had really stolen the money at the bank.

"Payback is hell. Is that it, blondie?"

"Payback for what?"

"Calling you a ditz."

"If the shoe fits..."

Austin growled, and it wasn't a pleasant sound. When he did catch up to her, as she was sure he would, pit bull that he was, it wouldn't be pleasant. But Maxie had always dealt with the unpleasant with a smile and a sunny disposition. Everyone always fell under her charm.

"Do catch me if you can, Austin."

With those taunting words, she slipped out the motel door and ran into the night.

3

AUSTIN HEARD the motel-room door close and he hit the bathroom wall with the flat of his hand. The sound of his growl reverberated in the small, enclosed room.

"Spider, my ass!" he yelled as he slammed his back against the same wall and slid down to the floor.

Duped like a greenhorn. Duped by blue eyes as deep as the ocean, soft skin and a husky voice. What a consummate little actress she was.

And what an idiot he was! All it had taken was her scream. It had gone through him like ice water. He'd immediately raced to the bathroom to see what could have happened to her. And when he'd seen her in that skimpy towel, her creamy breasts rising and falling with her panic, it was all he could do not to kiss those full, pink lips. The woman was well armed and very, very dangerous.

She'd also stamped around on his pride. He took his job very seriously and he'd never lost a skip once he had the person in his custody. Never.

It would take just a phone call to summon the police. He reached around to grab the cell phone where he had clipped it to his jeans, but his hand came up empty. He rose and looked around the floor and the tub, but couldn't find the thing.

He groaned with the memory of Maxie's hand at his waist. She'd taken the phone. "Son of a bitch!"

He closed his eyes and clenched his fists. Dammit. Damn little pickpocket thief. Damn you, Maxie. She must have plucked the phone off when she'd been wrapped around him like an octopus. It didn't help matters that he'd liked every minute of her hot little body pressed to his. Damn hormones and damn his weakness for blondes.

He eyed the door, but it looked really solid and his shoulder and torso still hurt like hell from the chair that had hit him in the bar. If he broke down the door, he'd have to pay damages out of the bounty he'd collect from Maxie and that would reduce the amount he'd have to send Jessica to France. He decided it wasn't worth the effort. He'd track her down in no time, once the housekeeper released him in the morning.

It HAD BEEN a long night with only himself as company, but as soon as he heard the hotel-room door open, he began banging. When the housekeeper removed the chair, he came out of the bathroom. The woman made the sign of the cross, grabbed her cleaning supplies and got out of the room.

Austin found his cell phone on the bed next to his duffel bag. He clipped the phone to his jeans and picked up the duffel bag, but before he could get out the door the phone rang.

"Taggart."

"Austin, when you getting in?"

"Manny, I told you the woman would be trouble."

"What happened?"

"I lost her."

There was complete silence on the other end of the phone.

"You what?"

"Are you going to make me repeat it?"

"No. I heard you. I just couldn't believe my ears. You've never..."

"I know!" Austin said savagely.

"Cut her loose man. I'll send someone else. I've got a killer for you to pick up. More your speed."

"No. She's mine."

"Sounds personal."

"Now it's personal."

"Is she as beautiful as her picture?"

Austin's palms began to sweat. "More. Ever tried to talk to an angel, Manny?"

"Once, in a wacky dream."

IT TOOK HIM a whole day to find out what direction she had run and his anger increased with each mile until he saw red. His mood darkened when he found a trucker who remembered that she'd asked for a ride to Mesa Roja. He swore vehemently when the *check oil* light lit up. Now, he'd have to waste more time finding a service station. He didn't want to risk damaging the car not only for sentimental reasons, but also because he didn't want to get delayed or stranded in New Mexico for neglecting a potentially serious problem. His regular top-notch mechanic in Sedona had an emergency and Austin had allowed someone else, someone he didn't know, to look at the car. The man assured him that the light was faulty and had replaced the wiring, but now Austin was worried that this mechanic had missed something.

All the while he waited at the service station, he fumed that he'd wasted a whole day and she'd gone back to the same place he'd found her? Was that a way to rub his nose in it or throw him off her hot little tail?

When this mechanic told him he couldn't find any problems, Austin got back in his car. With his hands tight on the wheel, he headed back to Mesa Roja to apprehend the little trickster.

SHE HEARD the flat of his hand hit the door before it banged open. All heads turned in the direction of the sound. He stood in the doorway. The wind whipped his dark hair over his forehead, sunlight played with the ebony tips and shot light all around the room.

His dark eyes searched like a hawk for prey and they hardened when they lighted on her.

She gasped. Just a day later and she'd forgotten how much energy crackled around him, how larger than life he was.

Then she focused on the look on his face. Had she thought it would be unpleasant when she saw him again? An understatement if ever there was one. He looked mad enough to spit nails.

And in those eyes was part of his ancestry, the kind of man who roamed the plains and lived off the land by sheer will and honest bravery.

He stalked into the room and went straight up to her. He put his hands on his hips. Heads turned and eyes focused on them. The man she was serving scooted his chair back away from Austin. "Is this some kind of joke?"

"If it is, you're not laughing."

His mouth tightened and he bent down so he could look her right in the face. "I'm laughing on the inside, blondie, and my sides are splitting. Can't you tell?"

Soothing him seemed more prudent than irritating him. "Austin. I can explain."

"Can you, now. Good for you."

"You're ticked."

"No. I'm beyond ticked. I've been pushed into the realm of irate."

"You were taking me back. You wouldn't listen."

"I don't have to listen. I'm a bounty hunter. That's what I do. I bounty hunt. I have papers on you that give me all the authority I need."

"I didn't steal the money."

He took the handcuffs from his back pocket and snapped them around her wrists. He pulled her outside toward his car, followed by a lot of people.

"Where are you taking her?" challenged a man with a large handlebar mustache.

Austin stopped; his whole body tensed. He glanced at her, and she shivered at the dangerous look in his eyes. He turned, placing her behind him. Here he was once again protecting his bounty so that he could cash in on her when they got back to Sedona.

"I don't have to answer your questions." He told the crowd of patrons who'd followed him into the furnacelike heat of the waning day.

"She's part of our town. We want to know."

"I'm taking her back to Sedona. Anyone want to try and stop me?"

The man who had spoken stepped forward, but Maxie didn't want anyone to get hurt. She stepped around Austin. "Handlebar, it's okay. It won't be long before I'm back." She heard Austin snort at her comment. "Don't worry about me. I'll be fine."

"Are you sure, Maxie?"

She smiled. "I'm sure, Handlebar."

He grumbled, but he stepped back. Finally the group disbursed and returned to the bar.

"Where's your boss? Doesn't she want to knee me in the groin again? Just for old times' sake."

"I didn't ask her to do that."

"Right. Let me get this straight. You've only been in this town for a month."

"Almost."

"Whatever. And you have these people eating out of the palm of your hand? You are good, lady."

"You think I'm some kind of a con artist?"

"I think you look innocent and act innocent and you have a conniving little mind."

"I thought you said I was ditsy."

"I'm reassessing that opinion, especially after you

tricked me with that spider attack and snatched my cell phone so I couldn't get out of the bathroom.''

"I do hate spiders.''

He pushed her up against the car and kicked her legs apart. Expecting the same treatment she got before, Maxie gasped when she felt the warmth of his hands on her ankle. With deliberate slowness he slid his hand up her leg to the juncture of her thighs and Maxie swallowed hard and closed her eyes.

He slid his hands over her buttocks and around her waist, spanning her middle with his two strong hands. She could feel the heat of his body, his heavy, harsh breath seductively against the back of her neck. Then he searched her torso, his hands whispering over her breasts until she wanted to beg for harder contact. She knew he was trying to intimidate her, scare her, but his touch did little to frighten her. It only made her more aware of him as a man, more aware of his strength and hard masculinity.

Maxie got her feet under her and turned in his arms. His stare was hot, intense. She found her voice. "You don't scare me. This doesn't scare me.''

"Then you *really* haven't got the brains God gave a turnip,'' he said hoarsely.

His hair was thick, rich and dark. She twined a lock of his smooth hair around her fingers.

His face was exquisitely masculine with a day or two of stubble, darkening the curve of his strong jaw line. His eyes were slumberous as if he hadn't slept well in a few days. Even with her bold words, Maxie felt a flash of panic. He was too close, and her fascination for him would only cause her trouble in the long run. His brown-gold gaze was shooting sparks, and she swallowed hard in the face of his dangerous good looks.

"What would I have to do to scare you?" he whispered, his whiskey-hoarse voice cutting across her nerve endings like a rasp.

A rippling of goose bumps lifted the hairs on her arms. Or maybe the shivers came from the way his brown eyes centered on her, flashing warm and alive in their intensity. Her breathing went shallow and she really didn't have an answer for him. There wasn't anything about this man that scared her. It was her own passion that frightened her down to her toes.

He closed his eyes and moved his thumb, grazing the corner of her mouth and stilling. Slowly, deliberately he hooked his thumb beneath her chin and tilted her face up. "What am I going to do with you?"

Maxie knew a cue when she heard one. How much could she throw this guy off-guard? Distracting him was now her number one reason for any intimate contact with him. It was very obvious to her that he was attracted to her. Besides she was dying to know how his mouth would feel and taste. With that thought foremost in her mind, she dragged his teasing, tantalizing mouth to hers. Excitement burst and seared through her. Oh God, she thought, this was a mistake. She should never have done this. What she wanted and what she could have were two different things. She could have him, only temporarily because for

them time wasn't on their side. But this felt too real,
too right. He was solid as a rock and just as immovable and she was as light as air and elusive. But none
of those arguments doused the heat that flamed inside
her as he wrapped his hand around her neck, using
his thumb under her chin to tilt her head back. With
a soft groan, she eased her tongue into his mouth.
The flames leaped inside her, running like liquid fire
through her veins, searing all the way to her soul.

A semi breezed by, blowing its horn and Austin
stiffened and stepped back, cursing a blue streak.

Maxie blinked up at him. Stunned. Dazed. Dis-
oriented. It was the first time in her life she could
remember that she was ever speechless. Her lips stung
and burned, and her mouth felt hot and wet and
ultrasensitive—sensations that were echoed in a more
intimate area of her body.

"I'm losing my mind," he said softly, and then
without further ado, he took her arm and put her in
the car.

"Would you mind if I took the time to get my
clothes?"

"No, but make it snappy," he said as he drove
around the back of the Lucky Star, followed her in,
and got her belongings. It took no more than ten
minutes and they were back on the road.

They drove in silence until Austin said, "Did you
go back there to rub my nose in your spectacular escape?"

"No. I thought about going to another town, but I

didn't really have the heart for it. Besides, I had a shift to do.''

"You think you're cute, blondie.''

"I went back to Mesa Roja because I like the people and I told you. I just need to stall. I can't go back to Sedona right now.''

"I know I'm going to regret this, but why?''

"I'll be convicted, which makes me a felon, and in the great state of Arizona they will not issue a felon a liquor license.''

"So?''

"We need that license to open the nightclub.''

"Can't Dorrie apply for another one?''

"There's not enough time. And if we don't open as scheduled, we'll lose everything we put into Firecrackers.''

"That's a good story.''

"It's not a story.''

"It's as good as the one about you locking me in a bathroom so you could skip back to the town that I caught you in because you had a shift.''

"You have a very closed mind.''

And she had a beautiful mouth, shaped for kissing. He knew firsthand. Don't go there, Taggart. She was a little con artist who flashed those baby blues to get what she wanted. He turned away disgusted with himself for even thinking about kissing her again. "So sue me.''

At the bar she'd refused to be browbeaten and refused to step back. She'd faced him like a little general and he couldn't help but admire her courage.

"You do have some spunk, blondie. Not very many people would dare shove me into a bathtub headfirst or otherwise. Not even stone-cold killers I've nabbed."

She turned to him. "I really had no choice."

He'd acted tough to build a reputation, a reputation that helped him keep his skips in line. But this woman was neither afraid of him, nor intimidated. In fact, she hadn't taken her eyes off him. Finally he asked with annoyance, "What?"

"You've gone after murderers?"

"Yes. I've apprehended murderers."

"Was that...dangerous?"

Not as dangerous as those baby blues looking at him as if he was some kind of a hero. "It's dangerous."

"Come on, Austin, can't you give me more detail than that? We have a long ride ahead of us."

He stopped at a light and turned to look at her. "Why would an angel want to know about such ugliness?"

"I'm not an angel and I..."

As she trailed off and their eyes connected, Austin's pulse faltered, and he felt as if his heart was being squeezed in his tight chest. An unexpected kind of intimacy buzzed between them, suspending time.

With time still weirdly suspended, Austin tightened his hands on the wheel, the sensation inside him disturbed his equilibrium and set his heart pounding hard in his chest. A honk of a horn behind them made him realize that the light had turned green. He started for-

ward and when he reached a cruising speed, he spoke,
"The guy was really mild-mannered. The kind of guy
you wouldn't suspect of hurting a fly. He kept to himself and didn't have many friends. He was arrested
late in the investigation when it was discovered that
he had been in the dead woman's apartment. With no
priors and a strong citizen's record, he got bail. Of
course, he skipped."

"And you went after him?"

"I caught the skip trace. By then the police had
discovered another unsolved murder that coincided
with the one in Sedona. They called in the FBI and
after more investigation discovered that this guy was
a serial killer."

"And you had no idea because you were pursuing
him for the bail jump."

"Right. I had no idea."

"What happened when you caught up to him?"

The memory of that dark night, the blood, and the
pain was something he didn't like thinking about.
"He used a knife. When I entered the hotel room
where I tracked him to, he had his latest victim tied
to the bed."

"Was she still alive?"

"Yes, thank God."

"What did you do?"

"I untied her and told her to get the hell out of
there and call the police. I went out after her to make
sure she made it to the office safely and he hit me
from behind."

"Hit you? Do you mean he knocked you out?"

"No. He stabbed me. It went through my shoulder."

Maxie brought her hands to her mouth, her eyes filled with horror. "Oh my god!"

"It could have been worse. I have a sixth sense. I don't know how else to explain it. I moved before he struck. The doctor told me that an inch the other way and the weapon would have gone through my heart."

"What happened after he stabbed you?"

"I brought him down. The police and FBI showed up shortly after that and they took him into custody."

"Did you get your bounty?"

"I did, but it wasn't the most satisfying part of that trace."

"What was?"

"Saving that woman's life. She had kids and a husband."

"I'm sure that woman was glad to be alive."

"So was I," he said solemnly. "So was I."

A short while later and he knew she was still studying him with those clear blue eyes, then they shifted to the tiny shield hanging from his rearview mirror. With her manacled hands, she pushed against the talisman. "What's this?"

"It's a warrior's shield."

"It's cute. What's it for? To protect you from evil spirits."

"Sort of. My grandmother's a medicine woman. She made the shield for me."

"Do you have a picture of her, too?"

"Look, I don't want to get anymore personal with

you than I have to." He was worried he was becoming more interested in the sweet Maxie than he should be. Getting personal with her would only cause him more problems. And those problems he didn't need. He needed distance.

She clasped her manacled hands together in her lap. "I've already seen the picture of Jessica. What would it hurt to see one of your grandmother?"

Outside the window, the harsh and starkly beautiful New Mexico desert flashed by in a long ribbon of gold. Did she have to sound so hurt? He just couldn't seem to resist her. "Why don't you look at the pictures of my whole family?"

"Why not?"

"I was being sarcastic."

"I know you were. It's a defense mechanism I understand, but I'd like to see them anyway."

"Why is it a defense mechanism you understand?"

"I wasn't exactly the proper daughter my mother would have wanted. Dorrie fit that bill pretty good, but I couldn't seem to stay clean. If I had on a white dress you can bet I'd be the one to find the mud hole."

Austin chuckled because he could see that pretty clearly.

"It's true. She would have loved to have had you as a son. I bet your suit was always spotless and you even cleaned up your room."

"There's nothing wrong with that."

"No, there isn't. But good manners and good character usually start with the parents or more importantly, since you're a man, your father. They brought you up right.''

''My parents tried to raise me right.''

''Do you have a picture of them, too?''

He wished she wouldn't glance at him with those soft eyes and tantalizing mouth.

''My father's dead,'' he said suddenly as if it could deter her from her probing questions. He felt almost powerless to stop her from getting deeper under his skin.

''What kind of answer is that? Either you have a picture or you don't.'' She swiveled in her seat to stare at him. He was highly aware of her gaze on him every second of the ride, but she didn't say another word.

It made him crazy.

It didn't help that he was also uncomfortably aware of her lightly tanned thighs, which he caught glimpses of every time he glanced at her. It was damn near impossible for him not to think about reaching out and sliding his palm over her velvet-smooth skin to feel the fit firm muscle beneath.

She pushed at his arm and looked at him solemnly. ''I'm guessing you do have a picture of your family.''

He leaned slightly forward. Keeping one hand on the wheel, he reached back for his wallet. Dividing his attention between the road and the open wallet, he found the picture and handed her the worn leather.

MAXIE TOOK the wallet, his nearness intoxicating her. She gave into the temptation to take a deep breath.

He smelled like something dark, decadent, and wholly forbidden. She looked down at the picture and her heart lurched. He looked just like his son. Handsome devil, tall, imposing and he dwarfed Austin's tiny mother. Yet, he had his arm around her in an oddly protective gesture. "Your father looks like he's trying to protect her from a threat."

"My dad was pretty old-fashioned. He didn't like cameras."

"Thought they'd steal his soul."

"My father was a warrior. He'd protect my mother's soul before he'd care about his own."

Maxie thought instantly that Austin was cut from the same cloth. "They look really happy." She couldn't think of anything else to say.

"They were. My father died while installing an engine in a Mustang. Heart attack."

"This Mustang?"

Austin swallowed hard. "Yes."

"I'm sorry."

"Don't be. He was a happy man. He loved his family more than anything."

"Sounds like he passed that love down to you."

"He did."

"I bet he was a good man. He also passed that down to you."

"You've known me for a little while, and already you can tell what kind of guy I am."

"I can. Your parents raised a good boy."

Her life had been simpler before she'd known of the existence of Austin Taggart, but that was before

he'd burst into her life with his seductive scent and
eyes that saw through all her barriers. Those shrewd,
assessing eyes seemed as if they could look right into
her soul. She already had this desperate need to lose
herself in his hot eyes. Another lure she had to fight.
She wouldn't get the time she wanted to get to know
Austin better. Her situation just wouldn't allow it.
That thought brought with it a regret that speared her
heart.

"My father didn't get a chance to finish the job.
I'm more than a little rough around the edges. My
mother…"

She looked at him, at his tight mouth, his somber
eyes. "Let's just say that my childhood wasn't idyllic
after my father died."

"What happened?"

"What happens to a lot of kids when their families
are shattered. My mother remarried. He's white. He
didn't have much use for me. They argued. I left."

"Where did you live?"

"With my grandmother."

She looked at the small shield hanging from the
rearview mirror that had been painstakingly hand-
wrought by his grandmother. It was sepia-toned with
simple fluid black lines that formed a buffalo in the
center of the shield. She must care for him a great
deal to construct such a lovely talisman for her grand-
son.

Maxie flipped the picture of Austin's parents over
so she could view the next photograph. It was a pic-

ture of a young Apache woman dressed in an elaborate beaded buckskin dress. "Who is this?"

Austin glanced over at the photo she held in her hand. "My grandmother on the day she celebrated the Apache Sunrise Ceremonial."

"She looks so young."

"She's about twelve."

"What's the celebration for?"

"A gift of spiritual blessings given to a young girl by her family when the girl reaches puberty. The ceremony is usually performed in the summer. If you flip that picture over you'll see a more recent photo of my grandmother."

Maxie turned the worn plastic over and gasped. The photo depicted a sweet, wrinkled, old woman with a slight smile, gray hair, and snapping black eyes. "Oh Austin, she's absolutely adorable."

When she looked over at him his face broke into a big beautiful smile. Their eyes met for just a moment, but the shared admiration for his grandmother seemed more intimate than the kiss they had shared.

"She is and she's wiser than Solomon."

"I would love to meet her. I could use some wisdom about now. Do you have any recent pictures of your mother?"

"Yes, the next one."

When Maxie reached that picture, she definitely saw where Austin got his good looks. His mother was stunning with big dark eyes, straight black hair, and a winning smile. "She's beautiful."

"Yes she is," he said, taking the wallet from her and putting it back in his pocket.

Austin lapsed into silence and they traveled along until they reached the outskirts of Cimarron, when Maxie spoke again, "Could you stop at a drugstore? I need some supplies."

"What kind of supplies?"

"Female ones," she said wryly.

"Do you have money?"

"Yes I do."

"Part of the money you stole from the bank?"

"I told you, Austin. I didn't take the money from the bank. I was framed. So, if you're expecting to collect the reward for discovering where the money is, you're going to be disappointed, because I can't tell you, since I don't know where it is."

Austin clamped his lips closed. As soon as they saw a drugstore, he parked the car. He unlocked her cuffs. "No tricks, Maxie."

She looked at him and raised her chin at his challenging tone. Austin felt like an ogre. He'd kill anyone who treated his sister this way. He tried to gentle his features. "Just hurry up."

Maxie nodded and walked into the store closely followed by Austin. He stood by the door as she walked through the aisles and picked up what she needed. He shifted a couple of times when he saw the male patrons in the store eyeing her. He didn't like it.

Suddenly a little old woman cried out and her basket toppled, spilling the contents into the aisle. Without thought, Austin bent down and helped the elderly woman pick up her items. She thanked him profusely. With a shot of adrenaline, he remembered Maxie and that she was loose in a store full of patrons with an available back door. He searched for her, but saw that she was standing in the aisle staring in his direction. He shrugged his shoulders and she gave him a little smile of approval.

She walked up to the counter and put down her items. The young guy behind the counter eyed Maxie intently.

"Is that *all?*" the clerk asked.

It was evident that the clerk thought she was attractive and she thought that was sweet. Maxie was delving in her fanny pack for her money when an idea came to her. It was a hasty, most likely ill-conceived plan, but it might just give her enough time to get away.

"No. I could really use your help." She fluttered her lashes all the while feeling guilty again that she would have to put Austin in an awkward situation and make him out to be some villain. But she was nothing but a paycheck to him and she was justified in doing this because she was innocent, and eventually she would prove it. Yet, those thoughts didn't seem to lessen the regret she felt. Damn. Why had she asked about his family in the car? She would have really liked to believe that he was a one-dimensional tough guy.

She also had to worry about Dorrie, Firecrackers and the terrible legal situation she had landed in. Austin would survive. "See that man over by the door? He's holding me against my will."

The clerk was a young male and, unfortunately, as soon as she mentioned Austin, he gawked at him with obvious distrust and alarm.

When Austin saw the clerk's face, his eyes narrowed. He moved forward, but the clerk slid around the counter and stood up to him. "You better leave mister, before I call the cops."

"Look junior, I don't have time for..."

"Is there a problem here?" Austin turned to find a deputy sheriff standing at his right shoulder. He was in a starched tan uniform that said *Deputy Shawn Miller* on the shiny pin attached to his chest. He was young, but looked competent.

"Arrest him, Shawn, he's a kidnapper," the store clerk said, pointing at Austin.

Austin's gut clenched. Oh, damn. What had the skip done now? Resisting an impulse to glance in her direction, he said calmly, "There is a misunderstanding here." Reaching back, he went to pull the bounty papers on Maxie, but his hand never made it all the way to his pocket as the deputy pulled his gun and pointed it at Austin.

"Keep your hands in plain view, Mister!" The man's hand shook and Austin wondered if this was the first time this guy had pulled his weapon. Staring down the barrel of the gun of a nervous, tense deputy shut Austin up.

"Slowly turn and put your hands on top of the counter." The deputy frisked Austin and then he took each of his hands in turn and handcuffed them. The cold steel sliding around his wrists made him look immediately at Maxie. She was watching him intently, her big blue eyes filled with...guilt. It surprised him for a moment that when the deputy hauled on his arm he didn't move. Guilt? He expected triumph or joy, at the very least gloating. But no, instead she looked at him as if this would be the last situation she could ever hope to see him in.

"Come on, Mister."

"There's no need for excessive force, deputy." Maxie put her hand on the deputy's arm. He too seemed to fall under her spell. Austin felt sick—he should be worrying about how he was going to keep Maxie from running, not about moon-eyed saps.

She smiled and had the audacity to look relieved to have the deputy there to protect her, as if Austin were a low-down kidnapper. "I was hoping I could call my family. Do you mind if I use the phone for just a second."

Austin immediately searched out the phone. It was close to the back door. "If you let her use that phone..."

The deputy shook Austin. "I told you to shut up." The deputy eyed him and then Maxie. "I think it might be better ma'am if you accompany me to the Sheriff's office. You can use the phone there."

"Look, if you just give me a chance to speak," Austin tried again.

"Save it."

In the patrol car, he once again tried to give the

deputy an explanation, but was told to wait until they got to the office, which didn't take long.

Once there, the deputy wasted no time in removing the cuffs and placing him in a cell. Maxie, Austin noted sourly, was helped into a chair as if she was an invalid.

Austin leaned against the cement-block wall and stared at Maxie through the strong iron bars. The jailhouse was modern and well-kept. Two narrow cells lined one wall. At the far end of the room, there was a table holding a coffeepot and a fax machine.

Near the door was a large bulletin board cluttered with posters and announcements. The sheriff's desk was modern and shiny, its surface strewn with file folders along with a neat stack of papers on the corner, a phone and a humming computer.

Austin focused on her face, then on her lips as they moved. Her damn mouth was so sexy, and he knew she pulled him into that kiss because she wanted to distract him. He knew it was a ploy, but it felt much too real to be fake. Just like she was faking her kidnapping story and using the deputy's hormones against him. If Austin wasn't jealous of the way the man looked at Maxie, he might feel sorry for the guy.

He would kick himself if he lost her again, that is, if she managed to make it out of this office without him yelling down the rafters. He was still about twelve hours away from Sedona, and their jaunt into the drugstore, which had landed him in a cell, was eating up precious time. The sooner he got this skip to Sedona the better for his libido, heart and temper.

She made him feel so many different levels of emotion. He wasn't sure which way was up anymore.

Austin jerked upright and went to the bars, his hands curling around the cold iron. If that man leaned over her one more time…

Just then the deputy rose and disappeared into the back room. Maxie was out of her chair and to the front door in two seconds flat.

With her hand on the knob, Austin was about to call out. But just then, she jumped back, the door opened and the sheriff walked through. The crestfallen look on her face gave Austin a little satisfaction. At least now he could get someone to listen to him.

"Well, what have we got here?" the sheriff asked, just as the deputy came out of the back room with a glass of water in his hand.

IT HAD TAKEN all of fifteen minutes to explain to the sheriff who he was, to get out of the cell and then out of the office. Maxie did a quick calculation in her head. Taos was two hours from here and then Albuquerque another three. She was sure he could make Albuquerque by nightfall. Then it was another eight hours to Sedona, a drive he could make easily in one day. She could be back in custody tomorrow.

Maxie was worried about the embezzlement charges. Since she'd been arrested, there wasn't a single day that had gone by that she didn't think about them. It was because of the arrest, that she was going to let her sister down. Again. She couldn't bear it. It was Dorrie who had taken her in when she'd been unable to cope at home anymore. And it had been her sister who had helped her get the bank job. How could she face Dorrie if the license was rejected and they couldn't open on time? How could she face her sister, knowing that everything they worked for, every minute of every hour they had toiled, was for naught. They would lose everything. To compound it all, Maxie would find herself convicted of a crime she hadn't committed and spend years in prison.

She needed more time. More time for Jake to discover the electronic trail the police barely bothered with when her co-worker accused her of embezzlement and they'd found her account filled with over a million dollars. And then that money had vanished. Been transferred again and even the police computer crime experts couldn't find it. Maxie had faith in her friend Jake and he'd told her to stall as long as she could. She had to stay hidden until he had a chance to follow the confusing trail, and clear her name.

When they were outside the office and headed toward the car, Austin took out the cuffs, but hesitated in snapping them around her wrists. She could see him remembering how the hard metal felt, the helplessness, the embarrassment. With a savage oath, he snapped the cuffs around her wrists.

"Not fun to be innocent and on the wrong side of the law. Now you know how I feel," she said softly, meeting his eyes head on.

"Is that why you did it?"

''No. I was trying to get away. You don't seem to understand my situation.''

''I've tried to tell you, blondie. I don't have to understand your situation.''

She resisted when he tried to load her into the car. ''Please, Austin. Let me go. I swear you can bring me in as soon as the license comes through.'' A bad case of the shakes hit her. Closing her eyes tightly, she acknowledged how scared she was now. So damned scared. Determined not to let fear overwhelm her, she made herself concentrate on taking deep breaths, making her muscles relax.

''I can't trust a skip trace. You must think I'm stupid. Manny has a lot of money tied up in you. You're going back now.''

''All I am is money to you. Why doesn't it surprise me that you care so much about the payout? I guess you wouldn't be in this line of work if you cared at all about people.'' The fear tightened in her gut, panic clawed at her throat. She wasn't going to convince him.

''That's a low blow and you know it. Caring about people has nothing to do with being a bounty hunter. This is a job. Pure and simple. I'm taking you in for jumping bail. Pure and simple. Now get in the car.''

The panic broke free, and she hit him hard in the midriff, knocking the air from his lungs. Before he had a chance to draw in enough air to catch his breath, she was hotfooting it behind the drugstore. He caught her near an empty loading dock. He reached out. She shied sideways in a desperate attempt to avoid his grasp.

He caught her again, her back against his hard, immovable chest. He wrapped his arms around her upper arms. In her haste to get away, she pushed backwards and he lost his balance, his back slamming into the wall of the drugstore.

Panting with exertion and fear, she pleaded, "Let me go. Please." She twisted in his grasp working with all her might to get free.

"It's all right, Maxie. It's okay. Calm down," his voice low and soothing. He turned her twisting body in his arms so that he could make eye contact. She pushed against his chest with her manacled hands. "Let me go."

"I can't, Maxie. I can't."

She collapsed against him. With a tenderness and concern that shocked her, he pressed her face into his neck, stroking her hair.

Closing her eyes against the sudden welling of tears, she clenched her jaw, feeling as if she were about to shatter.

She heard him swear. Then he gripped her chin, and brought her head up, forcing her to look at him. "Listen to me. I'm sorry that I was insensitive back there. The truth of the matter is you were right. It was uncomfortable being accused of something you're not. I didn't like it. And I do care about people, but I also have a job to do."

Startled into stillness, transfixed by his touch, Maxie stared up at him, the urgency of his words registering. She closed her eyes and forced herself to pull it together.

Focusing on what he'd told her, she met his gaze, showing with a small nod of her head that she understood. Austin eyed her, his eyes dark, and then he gave her head a gentle little shake. "Okay?" he asked, his voice soft and husky.

"I had to try to escape."

"I know. It's natural. There's always a place in the process of getting from point A to point B, when it's clear to a skip he's going back to face whatever it is he's run from. You hit that place. I understand your panic. And I'm sorry."

She nodded again, and when he tugged, she followed him back to the car. As soon as they were situated, he leaned over and unlocked the cuffs. "I guess while we're in the car you won't need them."

Something gave way around her heart and she shivered. Feeling almost too raw to speak, she reached out and put her hand on his forearm. "Thanks."

Austin stared at her for a moment, the muscles in his jaw hardening, and then he turned and hit the steering wheel with his fist.

Already weak from her panic attack, Maxie looked at him, her stomach dropping away to nothing. Not sure what to make of his behavior, she softly whispered his name. "Austin?"

He turned back to look at her, his expression tight, his voice harsh. "You are making this so...difficult."

He clenched his hands, a feeling of despair washed

through her, and she removed her hand from his arm. Lacing her fingers tightly together in her lap, she fought to contain the tears.

Austin shifted, and then he cupped her jaw, lifting her face, ''Don't, blondie,'' he whispered gruffly. ''Please don't.''

She looked up at him. Her eyes were awash with tears and Austin brushed his knuckles across her cheek, and then brushed at her hair. His expression etched with strain. He swallowed hard and continued to look at her, his eyes dark and tormented. Then, he let loose a long, shaky sigh. He adjusted the way he was sitting and pulled her across his legs, gathering her up in a tight, enveloping embrace.

Maxie slumped against him, unable to handle the chaotic feelings that rushed through her. His compassion was much too much to manage and she curled up in his arms, thrusting her wet face into the arch of his neck. He urged her head even closer, his breath warm against the side of her face. He didn't say anything.

The shrill ring of Austin's cell phone pushed them apart. He retrieved it, pressed a button and held it to his ear. ''Taggart.''

He listened for a moment, and then pinched the bridge of his nose, his voice strained. ''I got her. Another day and a half and I'll be back in Sedona.''

Sensing his immediate retreat, Maxie separated herself and moved over onto her own seat, anguish once again sweeping over her. The defenses were back up, and she was once again alone. She started to tremble when the cold steel settled around her wrists.

"I'm sorry, Maxie. I can't take any more risks."

WHEN THEY PULLED into Albuquerque, the largest city in New Mexico, it was late. The city sprawled over sixteen miles from the lava-crested mesas on the west side of the Rio Grande to the steep slopes of the Sandia Mountains on the east, and extended north and south through the Rio Grande Valley.

Austin was in a foul mood. Twenty minutes after passing through a deserted downtown, he stopped at the first hotel he came to. It was an elegant hacienda-style inn and looked comfortable enough.

So he'd had a lapse in judgment. Those beautiful blue eyes had filled with tears and he'd caved, but Manny's call had put him back on the straight and narrow. He looked over at her, but he couldn't help the pain he felt in his heart. He had to be tough though, because the little lady was good at playacting. He'd seen her in action in the Cimarron Sheriff's office. Who knew when her tears were genuine or just a fraud? Even though, he admitted to himself, those tears in Cimarron *looked* real. Oh, get a grip, Taggart. She was just a good actress and he'd almost fallen for it.

She bit her lip and looked out the window when he once again locked her handcuffs to the steering wheel. He left the car to pay for the room.

As he returned to her, his cell phone rang.

"Hello."

"Austin. I just got home for summer break. I thought you'd be home by now."

"Hey, brat. I had a little bit of a problem with this skip, and I'll be there the day after tomorrow."

"Is the guy dangerous?"

Austin laughed, but without any humor. "It's a she and she's very dangerous."

"Austin, please be careful."

"I just mean she's beautiful and treacherous."

"Oh, I see. She's dangerous to the heart and libido."

"Definitely the libido. I don't have a heart."

"Right, Austin," she said softly. "You were so mean when you put everyone else ahead of your dreams."

He rubbed the back of his stiff neck. "I take care of my family, Jess. They don't give medals for that."

"They should. So, you'll be here tomorrow?" The expectation in her voice made him smile.

"Yup. See you then."

"Bye, Austin."

AUSTIN UNLOCKED Maxie's handcuffs and grabbed the bags from the back seat. Once inside the spacious room, he dropped their things to the floor and dug out his toothbrush and toothpaste. He pulled her over to the bed, which was draped with a colorful quilt, and handcuffed her to the metal frame. The room had a table with an oak desk and two chairs to match.

"I have to go to the bathroom."

Austin sighed. He unlocked the cuffs. "Go ahead and you might as well brush your teeth, too."

While she gathered her belongings, he checked the

small, very clean bathroom, satisfied that the window was too narrow for her to squeeze through. He did worry that the room opened up to a courtyard, but when he looked out, he relaxed. It was an enclosed courtyard.

Maxie went into the bathroom and closed the door. After a few moments she came out. He swallowed hard. She was dressed in a pair of pink panties and a tank top without a bra. "Is that what you're going to wear?" He cleared his throat as his voice squeaked slightly. She was at it again. He was sure she was trying to distract him with this show of her sexuality. Yet, he couldn't help the way his body responded.

"Why? Does my lack of modesty bother you?"

He cleared his throat again. "Um, no. It's just that you really don't know me that well."

"I don't know you that well, but you don't get off manhandling women. You told me so yourself."

"So I did."

"Just think of me as a paycheck and it won't be so hard on you."

Austin frowned as she sat down on the bed and searched through her bag. He pulled out the cuffs just as Maxie opened up a bottle of lotion.

She looked up at him with those big, blue eyes. "Austin, my wrists are chafed. Couldn't I have a breather from the cuffs? You can see me through the open door of the bathroom. How far could I go dressed like this?"

He looked down at her reddened wrists and took in her attire again. Against his will, sympathy surfaced. It gnawed at his gut and made him feel—ah, hell—made him feel like a jerk.

Austin tried to play it off by shrugging, hoping she hadn't seen the pity in his eyes. He went into the bathroom, careful to keep the door open and her in sight. Shucking his T-shirt, he proceeded to wash away some of the filth and sweat of the two long days of tracking the angel from hell.

He heard her gasp and he turned his head. She was standing behind him, her eyes on his torso.

"Oh no, Austin."

He looked down and frowned. "What?"

She reached out and he held his breath with anticipation.

"The bruises." Her voice caught.

He looked down again and shrugged. She was responding to the huge bruise he'd received two days ago. It covered his shoulder and disappeared into the waistband of his jeans. "Took a hit with that chair."

Her fingers trailed over his shoulder and down to trace the strong ridges of his ribs, her touch whispering over his skin.

He gripped the edge of the sink, sucking in his breath when he felt her first soft kiss against the sensitive skin of his shoulder. Her compassion took him by surprise and he felt a twinge on his heart. But he ruthlessly squashed it. He wasn't born yesterday. He'd been alone most of his adult life until his grandmother, mother and sister had needed him. He gave, but he never took. It was too painful when the person he had depended on turned out not to be true. Maxie wanted to get away and she would use any means to do so.

"You don't have to pretend to care about the bruises." He couldn't trust her. She had made two attempts to get away from him just this morning.

"I'm not pretending. How could you think that?"

Red-hot sensation coiled in his abdomen when he felt the brush of her fingertips at his waist. His breath sucked in with a soft, startled sound and he closed his eyes against the tightening in his groin.

He grabbed her hand and drew it away from his body.

"I'm sorry. Does that hurt?"

He swore softly and tried to regain his control, marveling at how a woman could be such a mosaic of both virtue and sin. "Surely you can't be that naive. Do you know what you do to a man when you touch him, angel? It makes me hard, stretched-to-the-limit hard."

He stepped away from her as he snagged a towel off the rack and wiped his face. Maxie withdrew with one last look at his mottled bruises.

"I wasn't…"

"Sure you weren't. Save it."

Maxie looked at him with big, blue guileless eyes and he wanted to kick himself. Was it all an act? Did she know exactly what she did to him? She made him feel alive. Alive in a way that he couldn't ever remember feeling. Anger spiked inside him then and it worked its way to fury at the unfairness of life. Their situation made it impossible for him to explore a relationship with her. Although his body craved her, he wanted more than sex with Maxie. She made him want to lay her down on that bed and make passionate love to her. He wanted to stay in this room with her until the world went away. He wished he didn't have to take her back, but he knew what his responsibilities were and he always followed through.

He clamped down on the anger. It didn't help his situation—to wish for anything involving her. Nothing had changed. *Life wasn't fair* was something he'd learned when his father had died and his stepfather had treated him as if he was less than nothing.

"Thanks, Austin, for being so gallant in the bar and saving me from…" She let the sentence trail off, and gestured towards his torso.

"Why are you thanking me? You said you didn't need anyone."

"I would be stupid to think that I could have fended off those men. If that chair had hit me, I would have probably broken ribs. Are you sure yours are okay?"

She brushed her fingers over his ribs, pressing too firmly. He sucked in a breath at the pain.

"I had no idea. No one's ever been physically hurt before because of me and my schemes."

"I chose to step in front of the chair."

"Why?"

"It's my job to bring you in. That would have been compounded if you'd been injured."

"Right. I almost forgot. Don't want to damage the merchandise."

"Maxie, that's not what I meant."

"I know where I stand."

He tried to find a different subject since they were at an impasse. "So you've had other schemes?"

She looked up at him. "Yes. After college, I got into credit card debt. My sister bailed me out. I wanted to travel and I didn't think of the costs."

"Lots of college kids travel, Maxie."

"I went to Europe to escape."

"Escape?"

"From my mother. She never thought I would amount to much and she had no problem telling me that. Made me want to screw up even more. Dorrie was kind enough to let me move in with her when I was sixteen. Your father's dead and my parents have disowned me."

"So, you only have your sister to help you with this embezzlement problem?"

"Believe me. If you met my mother, you'd understand. They wouldn't even return my calls."

Austin's protective instincts kicked in and he wanted to pull her into his arms because she looked so forlorn. But was she telling him all this to play on his sympathies? One look into those compelling eyes made him want to say no. She wasn't lying. Yet, it wasn't his decision. He was duty-bound to bring her in.

"I never did what was expected of me. I was a great disappointment to my parents."

"I always did what was expected of me."

"No surprise there. Dorrie bailed me out a lot."

"I know about wanting to protect the ones you love, especially your sister. I'd do anything for mine."

She met his eyes and the determination there made him groan inwardly. "So won't I. I'm not going to stop trying to get away."

"Thanks for the warning."

"It's not a warning. It's a promise." She turned and left the bathroom. Settling on the bed, she started to apply the lotion to her wrists.

He finished up, thankful that brushing his teeth gave him an opportunity to compose himself before he went out into the bedroom. He pulled the cuffs from his back jeans pocket where he'd stored them.

"You don't expect me to sleep with cuffs on, do you? My wrists hurt."

He felt a twinge of sympathy for her, but he knew what he had to do. "You just told me that you promise to escape. If you think I'm going to trust you while I sleep, you are crazy."

Austin lay down on the bed next to her, placed one of the cuffs around her wrist, and then locked the other cuff to his own wrist.

It was quiet in the room. The only sound was the steady drip from the bathroom sink and the wind in the trees. Then Maxie spoke. "I bet you usually go to sleep about the same time every night."

"Like clockwork."

"Austin, sometimes it's fun to buck the system."

"That's what landed you in this mess."

"If I had stolen the money, then I guess I would be guilty of recklessness. But I didn't."

"You're on the run. That's reckless."

"To you it might be. But to me, it's my only alternative."

"You think you're impervious to getting hurt? I've got news for you. You aren't."

"I bet you're so uptight no woman would be interested in trying to get past that tough, 'don't-touch-me' attitude to really see what's inside. Does that work for you, Austin?"

"My love life is my business."

"Sounds like I hit a nerve."

"Good night, blondie."

She settled down and it wasn't long before she heard his deep, even breathing. She sighed. Turning towards him, she spied his cell phone on the night table. She debated all of two seconds, and gently leaned over him. He didn't even stir. What do you know? The big, bad bounty hunter slept like the dead.

She dialed. After three rings, a sleepy voice picked up. "This better be good."

"Jake. Sorry to call so late, but it's the only opportunity I've had."

"Maxie! How's it going?"

"Not too good. I got caught."

"Where are you?"

"Only a day away from Sedona, at the most."

"You've got to give me more time. I'm really close to tracking the money. As soon as I have a name, you're cleared. How many people had your account code to transfer this kind of money?''

''No one. We're supposed to keep that confidential and I didn't tell anyone.''

''Well, it was a good frame. It really looks like you did all these transfers, but I'm not giving up. I believe in you, kid.''

''I can't tell you how much this means to me, Jake. You are a true-blue friend.''

''Not really. I want an introduction to your sister.''

''You've got it.''

''Try to give me a couple more days. Once you're convicted, it will only be that much harder to win your release. God knows it could take years to get you out of prison.''

''Thanks again, Jake. I'll do my best.''

She disconnected the call, and was even more anxious now that she'd spoken to Jake. She had to escape Austin and she had to do it soon. She thought about it, then dialed her sister's number.

''Hello.''

''Dorrie, it's me.'' She looked at Austin, but he didn't so much as move.

''Maxie. Where are you?'' There was concern and love in her voice.

''You wouldn't believe me if I told you,'' Maxie said wryly.

''Try me.''

''Well, you know that guy who came into the bar a couple of days ago posing as a liquor license guy?''

''That gorgeous Native American. Yowza.''

"I'm handcuffed to him."

"What?"

"He's a bounty hunter."

"Oh, my God. What are you going to do?" Panic was working its way into her sister's voice.

"Get away from him, of course."

"You were always the wild one, Maxie. Please be careful."

"Is everything okay there?" Maxie asked.

"Sort of. The beer glasses are still not here. I'm still searching for a bartender, and the fire inspector isn't really happy with our electrical wiring. He thinks it all has to be replaced."

"I wish I could be there to help you. I'm sorry I caused us so much trouble, but I swear, Dorrie, I had nothing to do with the missing funds from the bank."

"I know you're innocent, Maxie. Has Jake come up with anything yet?"

"No. He told me to stall. He's confident that he can trace the money. He says a couple more days should do it."

"So is the bounty hunter letting you use the phone?"

"No. I'm using his cell phone."

"Maxie, I should start calling you moxie."

"He's asleep and he won't even know I used it. He's all gung-ho about dragging me back to Sedona to face trial for a crime I didn't commit. It gives me comfort to talk to the people who care about me."

"Be careful, Maxie. I do love you. Bye."

Maxie returned the phone to where Austin had left

it before he'd fallen asleep. She turned to get into a comfortable position and came face-to-face with Austin. His face was rough with dark stubble and there was a blatantly sexual droop to his full bottom lip. She thought of that moment when his lips had touched hers. It made her body hum. His dark hair on the white pillow, a sharp contrast. His long lashes, like crescent moons against his dark skin, looked soft and thick. She looked down the strong column of his throat to his heavily muscled chest and broad shoulders. Then the bruise caught her eye and she felt her heart soften that he had actually taken such a blow for her. Of course, the bounty on her was high, along with a large reward if he discovered where she supposedly had the money transferred. Money was all that was important to him, so what did it matter if she tried to escape him? What did it matter at all?

He had a job to do, as he was so fond of telling her. So, she shouldn't feel guilty about escaping or about the bruise on his body. She reached out and lay her hand on the mottled bruising on his ribs. She couldn't help wanting more time with him. It was a yearning that seemed to grow each minute she spent with him.

Glancing up at him to make sure she wasn't disturbing him, she traced the outside of the bruise. He was taking her back to Sedona for profit, yet she did feel very guilty about what he had done for her. It made her uneasy because she didn't want to care about this guy. It would be easier if he played the part of a villain. Easier for her to do what she had to do without thought to how her actions would affect him.

It was pretty clear to her that the guy slept like a rock. No wonder he was adamant about her wearing the handcuffs while they slept. Maybe she could use that somehow.

The remote was right on the nightstand and she reached over him and picked it up. She turned on the TV and smiled at the funny late-night talk-show host.

She checked Austin every so often to see if he was stirring, but he slept on, oblivious to her movements.

The bruise caught her eye again and she felt a tightness in her chest. He'd never hesitated when he blocked that chair from hitting her. A perfect stranger, one he knew as a fugitive from justice, and still he'd taken the blow for her, but she had to wonder if he was truly worried about his bounty being damaged. It would be much harder for him to get her across two states if she was injured. The incident only made her hunger for more information about this man.

No matter what he said with his ''don't-touch-me'' stance, she was convinced that deep down inside, he was as noble and honorable as the knights of old. She wasn't sure how she knew that. No one, it seemed, had ever given him much of a chance to prove it.

WHEN MAXIE WOKE, she eased onto her back, trying to slide away from Austin who had flung himself across her while he'd slept, his jeans pocket not far from her hand. Maybe he put the key to the handcuffs in there. It didn't make much sense, but she would be a fool to pass up such an opportunity.

She slid her hands between their bodies and went into the pocket and felt around. She glanced at Austin, but he was still asleep. She had to drop her shoulder to get in deeper.

"If you're looking for the key, I'd be pretty dumb to put it where you could reach it."

"I wasn't looking for the key."

"Sure," he said as he opened his eyes. "What were you trying to do then?"

"I was trying to get you off."

It only took a moment for her to realize what she had just said.

Austin's mouth kicked up into a wicked, genuine, all-out smile. It was beautiful and made her heart skip a beat. Then she laughed.

"I don't keep it in my pocket, blondie, but you're close."

She moved her hand slightly until she felt the hard heat of him and squeezed slightly. He hardened immediately in her hand.

Austin gasped and rolled off her. He gave her a level look and she just shrugged. "Don't dare me, sugar."

He flashed her a mocking smile.

"Could I take a shower?"

He eyed her for a moment. "Sure you can. As long as you know that trick won't work a second time." He reached down into his boot and came up with the key to unlock the handcuffs.

As soon as he'd unlocked the handcuffs, she got her stuff and went into the bathroom. She stripped and wrapped a towel around herself.

She pulled aside the shower curtain of the serviceable tub and let out a shriek and backed towards the door. But before she could go far, she came up against Austin's wide, naked, hard-muscled chest.

He grabbed her arm and spun her around. ''Maxie, I told you not to try it again.''

''I'm not. There's a snake in the bathtub.'' She simply couldn't hide the hysteria in her voice.

''I suppose it's a diamondback.''

''I think it is. I only got a glimpse.''

Austin sighed with a weary heaviness. ''Okay. I'll look in the tub.'' With one hand clamped to her arm, he pulled back the shower curtain. He snorted, reached into the tub, and came up with the snake. Maxie tried to back away from it, but Austin wouldn't let her go.

''It's a rubber snake. Nice try.''

''I didn't do it.''

''Sure you didn't.''

''Austin, I didn't put that snake in the tub.''

''Prove it.''

His voice had a note of smugness in it that made Maxie ready to do anything to prove to him that this time, she had really been preparing to take a shower. ''How?''

''Drop the towel.''

4

FOR A MOMENT she hesitated and he thought triumphantly, *Gotcha!*

But her eyes were full of mischief that suddenly made the mental triumph dissipate. Even before she reached for the knot of terry at her breast, the hair on the back of his neck stood up. He was, once again, in trouble.

His gaze followed the towel to the floor. He prayed she was wearing clothes. Please let this be another lame attempt to elude him. But when he raised his eyes, he let out a ragged breath, half sigh, half moan. The sound of it hung in the still air of the little bathroom, as pure and clear as the echo of a bell.

He should leave. He should obey his sixth sense and leave, except his sixth sense had ditched him just now. But he didn't really need it to tell him that a smart man would walk away from Francesca Maxwell, and every dangerous thing she awakened inside him. Maybe he just wasn't smart enough.

"Austin," she said softly as if he were held in some kind of mystic trance.

"Shhh, stay there," he said just as softly. "I'm looking." His breath caught in his throat as he let his eyes wander over her. She shifted as if his gaze burned, as if her heart was on fire. He stepped closer, compelled, feeling a burning in his chest. Was his heart on fire, too?

His hand rubbed at the spot where his heart was and her eyes followed his movement, making him want to groan again. Her hot blue eyes slid over him like silk over heated skin and he could barely breathe. His knees turned to water and a part of his passion-packed mind knew that he had never experienced such a sensation. Ever.

He breathed her in like she was delicate perfume. Exhaled her like heated breath. Absorbed her like skin absorbed the golden glow of the sun. Immersed himself into her like sliding into searing hot water.

She glimmered and shimmered like a flame before him, dazzling and scorching. He reached out, lost in the beauty, the mystery. He touched her face with his splayed fingers. Trembling with desire, he feathered golden eyelashes, her soft, startled mouth. His thumb dragged gently across her lower lip.

His gaze raked her body, his hand moving from her mouth to the tip of one pert, pink nipple. Gently he stroked the hot tip. It beaded up tight at the touch of his fingers, distending while the areola around it twisted and contracted until it all but vanished.

A low, rough sound of arousal rumbled deep in Austin's chest. He couldn't remember ever being aware of this kind of heat, this urgent need to sink into a woman in every way he could.

He shivered and stroked both hands down her sides

to encircle her waist. His fingertips nearly touched. His gaze lowered to the deep indentation of her naval, the full, sweet swell of her hips, and lower still to the thick golden delta above her long, firm thighs.

For one endless moment, time seemed to stop. Everything slowed as the need for her hung in the suddenly molten air between them. Silence rang in Austin's ears, then through the paper-thin walls, he heard the sound of running water, and outside the breeze picked up, causing a wind chime to ring. The soft sound did nothing to alleviate the edginess in the room. He believed that it couldn't have been disturbed by a hurricane. It only swelled and flashed hotter, closing out every sound, every movement, everything like a shielding wall.

With a soft curse, he jerked her into his arms, and then hissed through his teeth at the feel of her breasts flattening against his chest. Gripping a handful of those soft, spiky curls, he tilted her head back. He watched her eyes, those deep blue, mischievous eyes, as they glazed over, the color intensifying and deepening to a blue hot flame that took his breath away.

He wasn't the kind of man who took anything for himself. Not because he wasn't deserving, but because it so easily could be taken away.

For the first time in his life, Austin took and wished for a lifetime with her, so that he could experience this sizzling contact with her every day. Wake up to her every day. But time for them was fleeting, and soon he would have to let her go.

She shuddered as his lips claimed hers, her mouth

scalding against his. Her hand was in his hair and he closed his eyes against the wonderful feel of her fingers against the nape of his neck. It had been too long since he'd been touched like this, his responsibilities always overshadowing his needs and wants. His hunger was poised on a keen edge, the hold on his control tenuous at best.

When he raised his head, Maxie said, "Don't let me go. I'll fall."

"I'm already falling," he said huskily, and her eyes opened to look at him. She was a startling beauty with delicate features, her golden skin lovely, exquisite cheekbones and dark-gold-tipped lashes. She was gilt, sunshine, and he was finding it hard to resist her, just like he'd worried he would.

The desire in him roared and raged when he knew he had to let go of Maxie to keep his distance and his sanity intact.

"No," she pleaded, but his arms retreated and he set her aside, ignoring the smoldering desire in her eyes.

He knew that once he got a hold on Maxie, he wouldn't want to let her go. He'd experienced the searing pain of betrayal before—from his father, who'd died and left him to an uncaring and sneering stepfather—from his mother, too weak to stand up for him—from a woman he'd thought would be there for him, a woman who, like Maxie, was on the run and desperate to stay that way. Ready to do anything to get away from him.

He had to do everything in his power to keep

Maxie in his custody, turn her in to the authorities in Sedona, and collect his bounty. It wasn't just about his sister anymore and the money he needed to send her to France. This was about the dream that had been put on hold, since he'd promised to look after his mother, sister and grandmother. It's what a real cop would do. His duty was tied up with needing to do what his father would have done. He wouldn't have shirked his responsibilities. He wouldn't have been less than what he was. Even though his father was dead and buried, Austin couldn't shake the instinct to be like him. In a sense it helped to keep him alive.

He bent down and picked up the towel. He gently placed it around her and said, "Lift your arms." She obeyed and he pulled it tight and tucked in the end. His hands shook as he backed away, his heart aching with each step he took.

WHEN THE DOOR closed, Maxie felt as if she'd been drenched with cold water. He was stopping? He obviously wanted her. What could make a man turn away from a woman he wanted—a woman that was so obviously eager for his touch? Did he believe that she would try to trick him? Did he think this was a ploy to get away?

At first, she felt overconfident and smart-alecky when she'd dropped the towel to prove her point. But her plan backfired when she saw the look on Austin's face. When he'd groaned and touched her, Maxie had lost all her self-assurance.

Now she was aching and aroused and he'd so easily

let her go. She wanted him. They should be entwined and hot and sweaty by now. She went to the door and threw it open. ''It wasn't some kind of trick, Austin. I truly had nothing to do with that snake. What happened afterwards was not by design.''

''I don't deny that I want you, but I won't do it at the expense of my honor. Whether it was by design or not, I can't trust you.''

She walked up to him. With need coiling inside her, she slid her fingertips around his well-defined pectoral muscles and along the strong ridges delineating his abdomen.

There was something in his eyes, something that threatened to rip free. She wanted it.

As she moved closer to him, Austin boxed her in with his thick, sinewy arms, causing his biceps to flex and bulge. The quick-as-lightning movement halted Maxie abruptly, causing her to wobble. She caught herself by flattening her hands against the sleek expanse of his steel-muscled chest, her fingertips grazing and lying just below his tightening nipples. The sensation was like pressing against a rock-steady granite wall. Pure unadulterated lust stabbed at her, sending prickling heat skipping across her skin.

''Even if I were to enter you fast and hard like I want to, it's not going to change a thing. I'm still bringing you in.''

She should be more worried about what will happen if he made good on his threat and got her to Sedona. She should be intimidated to her very soul, but all she wanted to do was get closer to him. It was like a fascination for her—all that prowling energy trapped inside, yearning to get out. There was a savage edge to him hidden in the lethal lines of his body, shadowed in his bright eyes. He was no danger to her, though. She knew it as well as she knew her own name. The caged warrior would stay caged until she set him free. She shivered, thinking about all that energy unleashed.

"Right. The paycheck. I forgot myself there for a minute, but you didn't did you?"

"Go take a shower now. It's safe."

He meant she was safe from him. Well, she didn't want to be safe. She wanted to be wild and reckless. She dropped her hands. "What is it that you're afraid of? Making a commitment? Are you afraid that I'll hold sex over you?"

"Won't you, Maxie? Won't you use any means to get away from me?" he asked, his tone strained.

"Yes, I would. I can't deny it, but it doesn't mean that I don't have unguarded…moments when I wish we were just a woman and a man."

There was something in his eyes, hidden in the desire. Something she almost missed. It was regret. "It's more than that. More than just taking me back."

"I have to do my duty. It's what my dad would do. I can't succumb to temptation. There can't be any indecision on my part."

"Indecision? Are you having second thoughts about bringing me in?" Just when she thought she had him figured out, he changed the rules. It touched her that he wanted to be like the father he had lost.

Integrity wasn't something she thought she'd find in a bounty hunter, but she had to admit to herself that Austin was so much more than that. If he were anything less, it would be easy for her.

"Regardless of what you think, Maxie. I'm not insensitive to your situation, but I have no choice in the matter. Getting physical with you would just confuse an already bad situation. I have one act in this whole mess. To take you back."

Torn between the tenderness she felt for him and the intense fear that he would follow through with his threat, she couldn't argue the point with him. He was right. Having sex with him would complicate the matter. It annoyed her that he would have the steely resolve to carry out his convictions, but she couldn't possibly fault him. In fact, she felt her admiration for him go up a notch.

In the bathroom, she sagged against the sink, her knees weak with thwarted desire. She cursed him for having such amazing control. The tiny rational part of her mind told her that she had dodged a bullet, but the huge demon part of her wanted to push him hard to see how much effort it would take for him to lose it. She was sure Austin was ninety-nine-point-nine percent red-blooded male and only point-one percent saint. She was one hundred percent sure she wanted that hot-blooded male. With a frustrated sigh, she turned on the water. The heated spray loosened her tense muscles. Almost like hot, hard-stroking fingers. She closed her eyes and relived the moment when he'd touched her nipple. Pinpricks of heat traveled over her body down to her mound. Damn the man for having such incredible restraint. She turned off the spray and stepped from the bathtub.

She toweled off, went to her bag and rummaged around inside. All she had were tank tops, shorts and one pair of jeans. The jeans were out because of the heat. She chose a pink tank top and a matching pair of bicycle shorts.

When she came out of the bathroom, Austin was fully dressed.

''I'm starving,'' she said.

''When I checked into the Inn, the receptionist said they serve a buffet breakfast.'' She preceded him out the door and waited patiently while he stowed their bags in the car. Then they walked the short way to the main part of the hotel. He pulled out his cell phone and dialed a number. It was obvious he was talking to his sister and the way his features softened made Maxie's heart roll over. A tender feeling she pushed down because it was something she didn't want to feel, not if she was going to escape him anytime soon.

The waitress sauntered over. She was a tall blonde with very sensual features. She gazed at Austin with interest. Maxie felt her hackles rising.

Austin didn't even notice. He kept on talking on the phone. The waitress carefully placed the menu in front of him and the other one in front of Maxie.

Austin ended the call and the waitress smiled at him and he'd have to be blind to miss the sultry invitation.

"Can I get you something to drink?" she purred.

"OJ." He looked at Maxie.

"Just coffee for me."

"I'll give you a moment to look at the menus, then I'll be back...."

"We'll just take the buffet," Austin said, handing her back the menus.

"I'll be right back with your juice and coffee." She turned and left after giving Austin another appreciative look. Maxie's eyes followed the woman until she disappeared into the kitchen.

With his devastating good looks, women must constantly look at him, and her close proximity to him now was distracting her.

There were times when she knew he watched her, intently, his eyes glittering with heat. She wondered what it would be like to have him look at her that way for the rest of her life. Who was she kidding? It was impossible. Her situation was dire, complicated and terrifying. Besides, after he brought her back to Sedona and collected his bounty, he would be out of her life. She would face federal charges and with the evidence they had, she would be convicted. She didn't have any spare cash to hire a good lawyer and that would leave her with legal aid. Although her parents had money to burn, she'd rot in jail before she called them again, after being rejected the first time.

Suddenly, she felt the need to get away from him. Distraction was one thing, but getting jealous over a waitress was something else entirely. "I have to go to the bathroom."

"Leave your purse. Don't try anything, blondie. I'm not in the mood."

The bathroom had no escape routes. She figured he'd somehow already checked it out, and that was why he was so complacent. She felt dejected. She couldn't possibly get out the door without him noticing, unless she caused a scene.

Resigned, she left the bathroom and was greeted with the waitress conversing easily with Austin. The anger washed over her in hot waves, igniting her blood deeper and darker than was warranted. She tried to push it back and gritted her teeth. She knew why. She wanted to be able to converse with him in that easy way. She wanted to have a chance at a normal relationship with him. She pushed that thought away. The only place she was headed was jail and he was going to collect money for her after taking her there. There was nothing easy about that at all.

As she walked back, their waitress left just as another one passed their table carrying a large tray of food. She almost lost control. But with lightning speed, Austin was there, steadying the tray until she could gain control of it. The harried waitress turned her face up to his and thanked him for his help. She went on her way and Austin sat down. He stood up when Maxie approached the table and didn't sit until she did. She gave him an off-center smile.

"You have a chivalrous streak in you when it comes to women, don't you?"

The glance he shot her was abruptly wary. "Chivalry and women,'' he repeated, careful to leave all inflection out of his voice.

Maxie gave him a tender smile, for he clearly didn't want her to reflect on his character at all. Did he worry she might find a weakness she could manipulate? "Then why did you block the chair at the bar?"

"I told you I don't want my bounty damaged."

"If that were the case, why did you help that little old lady in Cimarron? And just now, you saved that waitress from losing all that food."

He shrugged and took a long gulp of his orange juice. "Just because I help out when needed, doesn't make me some kind of knight."

Maxie put her hands in the air and sat back, "Far be it for me to point out any good qualities you have, Austin."

She added cream to her coffee and took a cautious sip. "After all, you are the guy throwing a monkey wrench in all my plans."

"So you admit you have plans."

"I had to have plans. Innocent people who are being framed and then railroaded by the cops and the FBI need to watch out for themselves."

"It would be easier for you if you turned over the money."

"I don't have it. If I did, don't you think I would have skipped the country by now? Or at least bribed you with a portion of it?"

"I don't know your plans, Maxie. You could have

any number of contingency strategies up your sleeve. I hope bribery isn't one of them. It won't work.''

''I only have one hope. I have to stay away long enough for Jake to find out, through electronic means, who embezzled that money. When he has a name, and evidence, then I can return and clear my name.''

''So who is this Jake guy? Someone else you've duped.''

''No. He's a college friend who cares about what happens to me.''

It was obvious from his expression that he was skeptical. ''You don't believe that someone could have concern for me?''

''Maxie, with your face and body, it would surprise me that all a guy was interested in was concern for you.''

''Jake has no interest in me romantically. I think he's sweet on my sister.''

''Good for him.''

''Dorrie has sworn off men. She doesn't trust them very much since the last guy she was involved with broke her heart.''

''Not all guys are bad.''

''I didn't say they were. I said Dorrie thinks that, not me. I happen to think most guys are pretty decent.''

''Let's get to that buffet and then we're out of here.''

She rose when he did, but she grabbed his forearm. ''Austin if you take me back, I could lose everything. I can't let my sister down. Please.''

"Blondie," he said, covering her hand in a gesture that startled her. "I told you why I couldn't. I haven't changed my mind and I won't."

Maxie sighed and preceded him to the buffet line. What she needed was a miracle. An honest to God miracle.

"DAMN."

Maxie looked over at him as he peered at the dashboard. After they finished their breakfast, Austin had wasted no time in getting her to the car, but for some reason he hadn't bothered with the handcuffs. Now, he was looking dead ahead and swearing. "What's wrong?"

"The oil light is on again."

"Is that a problem?"

"It is if I don't want to break down in the middle of nowhere down the road. We still have about eight hours before we pull into Sedona. I even had this checked before I left and on my second trip to Mesa Roja. One mechanic said it was a faulty light, and the other couldn't find anything wrong."

"What are you going to do?"

"Go to a garage."

Maxie felt a glimmer of hope blossom inside her. Maybe, just maybe she was getting a second chance and this was the miracle she needed.

It didn't take more than ten minutes to find a garage and another ten to find out that Austin now had a serious oil leak on his hands that wasn't detected in Sedona or Raton. She didn't understand all the mechanical mumbo jumbo, but it was obvious to her that it was serious enough to keep them in Albuquerque overnight. She wanted to crow her delight to the heavens. It would give her time to find an escape route. There was a modest, one-story motel across the street from the garage, constructed of stone and adobe with a pitched roof. Austin grabbed their bags out of the car and took her wrist as they crossed the four-lane highway.

After checking in, they got the key to the room. Maxie rubbed absently at her wrist as they entered the medium-size room with clean lines and a comfortable-looking bed. Outside the window was a small park with a pool. People were around it, enjoying a cooling swim.

Austin threw the bags on the bed. Maxie went to her bag and pulled out the lotion. Suddenly he was there, hovering over her.

He looked at her wrists and then at the lotion, his eyes dark and intent, his jaw tightening. Just like that her knees grew weak, and it was all she could do to keep from losing her equilibrium, and letting sensation sluice over her with a poignant richness, letting herself get lost.

He took her wrists in his hands and studied them. With a soft curse, he took the bottle from her. His big hands were gentle as he poured lotion into his palm and applied it to her wrist with soft strokes. His touch set off a new surge of weakness and she closed her eyes, overwhelmed by the pulsing need that made her heart pound and her lungs seize.

He was quite the man of contrast. He said he'd gone after murderers and she bet other dangerous people, yet his big hands were so soothing and tender. She hoped he had some means to protect himself. Why that mattered to her at this moment she couldn't understand.

"Do you have a gun?"

His head came up and he frowned. "Why?"

"You said you'd gone after murderers. I bet there've been other dangerous types, too. Aren't bail enforcers allowed to use guns?"

"Yes, in most states."

"In Arizona?"

"Yes. I carry a gun, but I don't like using it. If you start off with violence in catching a skip, then where do you go from there?"

"Yeah, I guess they don't go for the 'bring 'em back dead or alive' concept anymore."

"No. They frown on dead. No one wins then. I like to rely on my street smarts and intuition. Bounty hunting is just really common sense."

"In what way?"

"There are a lot of reasons wanted people run. First and foremost, they don't want to go to jail. Some run because they're afraid, and others because they're trying to hide from other charges. Most think they can get away with it. I always go to family first. It's a given that when people are threatened, they'll seek their family's help."

Even though the lotion had been absorbed into her skin, he still stroked her wrist. She could feel the goosebumps, and she used a question to try to distract her from his caress. "So that's why you went to Dorrie first."

"Sure, it made sense you would keep in touch with your sister. You had a pending liquor license, you own a nightclub together. There were many reasons I believed that you would have some contact with your sister."

"So you put yourself in my place?"

"Yes, if you want to be successful at this job, you have to know how to hide. Once I apprehended a skip by using the phone because time was imperative. I only had two days before the bounty ran out. I had to get other bounty hunters in different states to help out, but it was cost effective and successful."

"The modern-day bounty hunter. So before me, you've never lost a skip?"

"No. Never."

He was going to have to get used to it, because Maxie had no intention of getting any farther away from Mesa Roja. He was about to lose her again just as soon as she could figure out how she was going to do it.

5

"SINCE WE'RE STUCK here, do you think I could wash some clothes? I haven't anything clean for tomorrow and I would really rather not face everything in rumpled and dirty clothes."

She was now a day away from Mesa Roja, and she vowed she wasn't going to get any farther away. It was time to plan an escape from her captor. But how?

She had no intention of being here tomorrow morning to continue on to Sedona.

"That's not a bad idea. I'm out of clean clothes, too. I didn't think it would take this much time to get you back."

Austin picked up both bags and they went to the small washing alcove not far from their room. Detergent was provided in vending machines and Maxie got what she needed. Austin had already loaded a machine with his clothing. "I can't see wasting water and detergent on washing two small loads when we could combine our clothes," she suggested.

He nodded.

She loaded the washing machine with her garments and got the machine going.

"What do you want to do now?"

"Go back to the room and wait."

"Wait. How boring. Can't we do something?"

"This is not a vacation."

"I know that, but do you want to sit around and look at each other?"

"It's safer than having to worry about losing you in a crowd."

They went back to the room and checked periodically on their clothes. Maxie got a jolt when their wash was on the motel-room bed for folding. Her unmentionables mixed in with his T-shirts and jeans seemed so very intimate.

While folding their meager garments, Maxie turned on the television. A Spanish soap opera appeared and she watched it as she separated the clothing.

A commercial interrupted the show while she put her clothes back in her bag, moving aside her small cosmetic case. She'd forgotten she'd left the zippered bag open in her preoccupation with Austin this morning. The bag spilled its contents onto the coverlet of the bed and Maxie reached to pick up the half dozen items. Her hand closed around the over-the-counter sleep aid she'd purchased. Due to the stress of her situation, she'd been having a lot of trouble sleeping lately. Her hand stilled. She glanced over at Austin, but he was engrossed in a magazine and didn't look up. She tightened her hands around the pills and knew how she was going to escape.

She bided her time until it was dark, and then she let it be known that she was hungry. True to form,

Austin wanted to stay close to the room, so he ordered out.

It wasn't long before the food came with Maxie's chance to get away. While he was in the bathroom, she opened one of the capsules and secreted the powder into his drink. The white granules disappeared without a trace.

Now, it was time to distract him and keep him talking, until he passed out and she was home free. She needed a topic and an obvious one came to her.

"Why a bounty hunter?"

"Why not?"

"Come on, Austin, don't be flippant."

His long lashes veiled his honey-colored eyes. "Do you think I enjoy being a bounty hunter?"

"I don't know, do you?"

"No."

"Then why do it?"

"There aren't a lot of prospects for a guy with a high-school education, a stint in the military and too few college credits under his belt. I needed money and I needed it fast." He avoided her gaze and dug into eating his food.

She said softly, "For your family, right?"

Maxie was sitting in the chair next to the bed. It was a tight squeeze with Austin's legs almost touching hers. "It's not a crime to love your family."

Guilt washed over her in waves. Maybe she didn't want to know this, not while she was trying to escape. But the look in his eyes made her hunger to know more about this stoic, tough-as-nails man.

"So why do you need this bounty so badly?"

"I need the money."

"I guessed that. What do you need the money for?"

"You just don't give up, do you?"

"Nope."

"It's for Jessica's education. She has the opportunity to study in France. She's a very talented artist."

Maxie felt as if someone had just kicked her in the solar plexus. He was going through all this for tuition money for his sister's education? Struggling against the sudden thickness in her chest, Maxie tried to camouflage the unevenness in her voice when she answered. "Why do you feel such an obligation to provide for her when her father is alive and well and should be forced to pay?" she asked, her tone gently challenging.

He jerked his head up, his gaze riveted on her. She forced herself to stare into his eyes. He reached over and picked up his drink. She wanted to grab it and stop him from ingesting any more of the sleeping aid, but she had to harden her heart. This was the only course of action she had open to her. Austin wasn't going to let her go. She had to escape.

She experienced a painful little twist when he took a few swallows of the drink. "It's true that I should force her father to pay, but I don't want anything from that jerk. He abandoned Jessica and my mother." He rubbed at his temple. "I went to the reservation and met my kid sister for the first time. She's much younger than me.'' He stopped talking. He shook his head as if trying to clear it.

''I remember the day I walked up to the shack they were living in. The first time I laid eyes on her.''

''Why was that the first time you saw her?''

''She's my half-sister from the union of my mother and stepfather.''

''Go on.''

''I was angry that I'd lost touch with my mother. Angry that I hadn't thought to find her and see how she was doing. After my stepfather left, they returned to the reservation.''

Maxie couldn't stand the self-reproach in his voice. She sat forward in the chair, brushing against his knees. Reaching out she put her hand on his bare forearm. ''It's not your fault.''

''I felt responsible. I joined the army after high school. It doesn't pay much, but I was well fed and sheltered, while they were destitute. My mother needed to see a doctor and both of them hadn't been eating enough.'' His fist clenched and he dropped his hand to his side. ''I wanted to kill my stepfather for his neglect and abandonment.''

''So you supported them.'' Maxie prompted in her vain attempt to steer him away from reliving that anger.

''I needed a lot of money fast. My M.P. training prepared me for law enforcement, and I could have gone to the police academy, but bounty hunting was more lucrative. I took on the more dangerous criminals, sometimes ones that other bounty hunters wouldn't touch. When my mother got better, she got a job and helped out. Then, my grandmother got ill and we also took her in. She wanted to sell her crafts, so we all moved to Sedona.''

"But, Austin, it sounds as if they're not dependent on you anymore."

"I have an obligation to them."

"Austin."

He scarcely heard her. "I would do it all again to save them. I would give my life for them. They mean the world to me."

"Austin, please don't."

"I want you to know that I understand your bond to your sister, but I have no choice. This is the way I support them. This is a job. They are my responsibility."

And she wondered what hopes and dreams he'd had to put aside to support a family he obviously loved.

"What did you have to give up?"

He looked at her skeptically, the knowledge that she'd read him so well clearly shook him. She could see it in his surprised eyes.

He swallowed and put down the carton of Chinese food. He shifted on the bed and his knee bumped hers. He breathed. She breathed. His slightly out-of-focus honey-colored eyes met hers, exchanging meaning, awareness, intimacy and knowledge, which she fought.

And lost.

She shouldn't be probing him right now. It wasn't

fair. He was losing some of his inhibition because the medication was starting to take effect. Why oh why couldn't she have met him in a more normal environment? Then, perhaps they would have had a chance to build something strong and lasting. Her time had run out and she felt a reluctance to leave. But, of course, she had no choice. She'd never had a choice from the moment they came to her home and arrested her for a crime she hadn't committed.

"I wouldn't ever turn my back on my family. Sometimes I…"

He trailed off as if he suddenly realized he was revealing more than he had to anyone in his life. He looked at her again with a dazed look in his eyes.

"Resent them?" she guessed, probing his eyes with her own.

He looked away and sighed. "In unguarded moments and never for long. They need me."

"So what did you give up?"

"The FBI."

"A G-man?"

"Yeah. I thought that being part of the law enforcement agency that protected the whole of the United States would be something that my father could be proud of. There was really no contest between a job and my family. It was tough to give it up, but it was worth it."

"Was it a job or a dream, Austin?"

"More a dream. But it didn't work out."

"Why did you have to give it up?"

"My family is tied to the land, and the training was in D.C. I couldn't leave them."

"I'm sorry."

"Do you know," he said "that my first bounty took me all the way to Washington. I must have stood outside the FBI building for almost an hour. I stood there and watched agents going in and out. I did feel regret. A sea of regret and then I was ashamed of myself."

"Oh, Austin, I'm sorry you had to give up so much." How was she going to go through with this? She'd had no idea he'd sacrificed this much for his family. His very dreams. Closing her eyes, she pressed her hands against her forehead, the horrible sinking sensation made her feel sick inside. Paralyzed by a horrible, churning feeling, Maxie wanted to cry. She whispered, "Where have you been all my life, Austin?"

"I don't know."

A stark realization hit her. Dorrie was a lot like Austin. There wasn't a time in Maxie's memory that her sister hadn't stuck up for her. "You make me realize how lucky I am to have my sister to help me out of scrapes. Selfishly, I never thought about how she struggled to help me." Afraid she was going to cry, Maxie wrestled with the tightness pressing down on her chest. And regardless of the pain she felt in duping him again, it firmed her resolve to do what she had to do, so that she wouldn't let her sister down. "I wish we could have met under better circumstances."

He slid off the bed and knelt on the floor in front of her, startling her with his nearness. ''You mean that?''

''I always say what I mean.'' Her need to comfort him overwhelmed every other thought in her head. He took everything so seriously, and she felt regret that she wouldn't get a chance to find out why. Something in his past had made him that way and she hungered to find out everything that made him the man he was.

He smiled and her heart suspended in her chest. She'd seen him give her a tight smile, a sexy, teasing smile, and a sarcastic smile, but this smile was genuine. It came deep from inside him, lit his eyes and literally took her breath away.

Hunger, deep and fierce, gnawed at her bones. Pleasure, sweet and lingering, full of anticipation made her insides turn to mush. Impossible emotions careened inside her. It seemed as if she hadn't been alive until this moment—this wonderful moment.

His eyes darkened and he leaned forward, his hips bumping against the edge of the chair she sat in. ''I want to stay away from you, but I can't seem to help myself.''

Her arms slipped around his shoulders, hands slid beneath his hair, cupped the back of his neck.

Her fingertips enjoyed the hard contours of his muscles, the smooth, male feel of his hot skin so wonderfully different from hers.

Her nostrils flared at the scent of him. The spicy masculine smell was quite sexy. She breathed him in and let him wash through her lungs, relishing his scent, savoring the flavor.

Strands of his hair brushed the backs of her hands. She moved her eager fingers through the thick, glossy tips.

Her breasts felt full, tingling, and her breath caught and held at the sensual promise. Her fingers tightened in his hair. Want skipped through her pulse, sent hot, jumbled need along her nerves, and trembled in her lungs. Her only coherent thought was that she wanted him even in a temporary way, even though, right now, her heart was full of him and what he'd done for his family. She wanted to pretend it was just sex, but she knew deep down in her heart it wasn't.

He rose and brought her up with him, against him, belly to belly, breast to chest, heart to heart. Oh damn, she couldn't do this. She should break away and insist that they sleep—do something. But she couldn't seem to, and as the guilt intensified inside her, so did her need for him.

As if he sensed her inner turmoil, his arms tightened around her, and his hands slid down her back to her hips and lower, pulling her against him, trapping her safe inside the dangerous embrace. His lips brushed along her cheekbone and he made a deep, rumbling sound.

His hot tongue traced errant patterns toward her ear. Awareness buzzed through her and made hungry, stabbing forays into her breasts, her belly, between her thighs.

Again that rumbling, deeper and more urgent this

time. His mouth became more restless, tongue more voracious, hands more bold, cupping her buttocks, and pulling her tight against the hardness of his erection. Lost in the spell, the moment, she arched her neck into his mouth and turned her face slowly toward his.

His cheek was hot against hers, his mouth voracious and inviting. She wanted it on hers, now, this instant, wanted thoughtlessness and total sensual devastation and plunder.

He took her mouth and all thoughts spun away. She forgot about escaping, forgot about her sister, her problems and on-the-run status. She forgot her own name.

Pleasure, deep and sinking, was melting her bones and turning her muscles to jelly. Hunger, hot and intimate, impatient, burned away inhibition. The world was elusive and distant. For now they were all that existed, and she existed only where their mouths meshed and clashed; where his arms fit around her, squeezing her tight; where hers clung to him. Their bodies tried to get even closer.

Their lungs shuddered and trembled trying to catch enough air. Pulling their mouths away to breathe, Maxie's insatiable fingers tunneled Austin's hair away from his face, caressed his neck, his cheek, his chest. "This isn't a good idea," he said his voice breathless.

"No," she agreed, trying to think while his furious hands swept up her sides to the outside of her breasts, sliding away.

Maxie pressed closer, lifting her chest, inviting his touch. "You'll still bring me in."

"Yes."

"I wouldn't expect anything less." His thumbs traced her jaw, moved with slow precision down her throat, brushed the curve of her breasts, skirting the fullness and the center and avoiding the crest with a sensual teasing that almost made Maxie come out of her skin. Moaning, she slid her hands roughly down his chest, around his sides, brushed his hips.

"I want you."

Groaning, Austin squeezed her to him hard. "Yes."

She eagerly opened her mouth under his. He thrust his hot, velvet tongue between her teeth and she met him with sensual movements of her own. Bringing her thigh hard against the aching demand inside his jeans, his hands slid down, rounding the slope of her buttocks. With a moan, he pressed himself to her with what felt like an uncontrollable rocking of his hips.

It drove Maxie crazy and she couldn't get enough of him as her hands moved mindlessly over him, touching him everywhere. Beneath his shirt, the hard muscles of his chest were smooth and tantalizing to her touch.

Somewhere deep, something sizzled inside her, bringing with it a tingle of fear, an intense appreciation of danger. She had an enthusiastic craving to take risks, command the flame with her naked hands, make it do her will and bring Austin into the flame with her, immerse him until he was burning, incandescent, one with her.

It was a familiar sensation, this untamed part of herself. Yet, recklessness never came with this brand of fear—this intrepid fear of getting caught in her own desire, of needing too much. Austin was the seducer and the savior for both the fear and the need. She'd known that the minute she'd laid eyes on him, known sooner or later that he was the man that could take down her defenses and leave her emotions bare, while he forged a path to her soul.

He'd become part of her thoughts without her consent, her knowledge.

But it was only sex, not a commitment, not a hope. Only sex. She had to believe it. And let it become emblazoned on her heart, because she needed to believe it, even if it was a deception.

For the moment, tomorrow's inevitable repercussions and pangs of conscience could take care of themselves. Now was all that mattered.

Getting closer to him, feeling the flame that had been waiting for the torch. Waiting for him. Losing herself in him, with him deep inside her.

She moaned and undulated beneath his sensual assault. Her body was a tome and she told him with her movements all that she wanted from him.

He wobbled suddenly and then sat down heavily on the bed, bringing her with him. She straddled his lap, frantic for contact, oblivious to his loss of motor control indicating that he was losing his battle with the medication in his system.

He slipped his hands beneath her tank and ripped the top from her body. With a deft movement, he unsnapped her bra. ''Damn'' was all he said as he stared at her.

His fingers brushed over her collarbone, tracing the long crease where the outer slopes of her breasts rose away from her rib cage, brushed his fingertips down to the indentation of her waist, and then trailed them over the flare of her hips.

''I want to see you fully naked again. I can't stop thinking about that,'' he said. ''I want only skin between us.''

''Yes,'' she said softly, and more sharply as he sucked her left nipple into his mouth. Another moan escaped her as she arched her back.

When he released her, she reached down and took off his T-shirt, pushing him back onto the bed.

Using her knees for support, she slid her groin against his and heard him gasp. Her hands went to the heavy muscles of his chest.

Running her hands all over that hard, hot male muscle made her hips move harder against him. She trailed her hands all the way down to the waistband of his jeans.

''Austin, do you have any condoms?''

He didn't answer her. Her hands stilled on the button of his fly and she looked up at him. The light illuminated his face, his eyes closed.

For a moment she stared stupidly at his face, his heavy, even breathing and it hit her. He was asleep. How could he have fallen asleep in the middle of…oh, damn.

He was out cold.

And she was so very hot.

His body was warm between her thighs. Hard, masculine, and she wanted that promise.

Her purpose came rushing through her as she got off his lap, picked up her pink tank and struggled into it. What had she been thinking?

"You'd be on top of him right this minute, taking all that hard masculine promise inside you. That's all you were thinking about."

In sleep, his face was peaceful and young. Did Austin carry pain around inside him and refuse to enjoy life because of that pain, or was it just his nature? She wanted to know desperately.

She tried not to feel guilty for deceiving him once again. She had to get away.

She went into the bathroom and grabbed her stuff. Back in the bedroom, she covered Austin as best she could, trying to ignore the tingling in her fingers each time she touched his bare skin.

Then she turned and started for the door. Overcome with regret, she stopped and turned around. She went back and leaned down. Very gently she kissed his mouth, caressed his cheek, and guiltily closed the door behind her.

The darkness covered her as she made her way to the highway, but she couldn't hide from herself. No, she saw herself very clearly.

And she didn't like what looked back.

"MAXIE, COULD YOU take this basket over to Mrs. Granger?"

"I'd be glad to." Maxie picked up the basket of

foodstuffs and turned to leave the bar. Star began to wipe down the counter and stack clean glasses for the night's revelry.

Handlebar walked in, spied Maxie and made his way over to her. "Hi, Maxie. I hope I'm not too late to donate to Mrs. Granger's basket."

"I was just on my way. You know how she likes to take in the night air and converse on her porch."

"I sure do." He placed a package of fancy coffee in the basket Maxie was carrying.

"It's really sweet of you to take such good care of an old lady," Maxie said.

"She taught most of us in this town. She's a nice person. It's the least we can do."

The whole time that Handlebar talked to Maxie, he stared at Star, moving around the bar. The woman was wearing a tight black sports bra and a pair of skimpy white shorts. Her dark red hair was pulled back into a ponytail that reached all the way to her tiny waist. And Handlebar couldn't take his eyes off her.

"Star's a good person, too," Maxie said, watching Handlebar's rapturous face.

Maxie continued when he didn't answer. "With a big heart." Finally he looked at her.

"Those star tattoos are pretty impressive, too," he said, smiling wolfishly.

Maxie elbowed him in the stomach to get his attention. "She's not going to know you like her, Handlebar, until you get up your courage and ask her out.''

"What would such a fine, sweet thing want with a tough guy like me?"

"Star? Sweet? Did you see what she did to that bounty hunter? He was walking sideways for a bit.''

Handlebar laughed and ruffled Maxie's blond curls. "Get on with you, girl. Mrs. Granger's waiting for you, I'm sure. You know how she loves her conversation.''

It had been three days since she had left Austin in the Albuquerque motel room. With guilt and remorse riding her hard, it had taken her a day and a half to get back to Mesa Roja. A kind trucker had let her hitch a ride and sleep in the back of his cab.

She walked out into the sultry New Mexico night and turned to Star's Harley. She secured the basket on the back and fired up the bike.

For a moment she sat in front of the roadhouse bar and thought about the potential this place had. It was close to the highway and even though it was a place where tough guys hung out, Maxie could envision it being more a place for the whole town to gather—rowdy guys at night and a family place during the day. All Star had to do was change the sign, put on a nice coat of paint, add a place to move the pool tables and dartboards. It really wouldn't take much effort. She was beginning to develop a soft spot for the Lucky Star. She shrugged her shoulders and wheeled the bike around, accelerating when she hit blacktop. Maybe she'd mention it to Star and see what her employer thought.

It felt good to get out of the dimness of the bar and let the wind of the bike clear away the cobwebs in her head. She'd called her sister last night, telling her of her latest escapade. Dorrie had feared for Maxie's safety once Austin tracked her down again, but Maxie wasn't afraid of Austin. And she assuaged her conscience with the fact that he'd wanted sex from her, so all she had done was to trick him and use his own passion against him. Somehow she wished she could make herself believe that, and be convinced that all *she* wanted from him was sex.

She'd also called Jake, but had found out that nothing had been resolved. Jake still couldn't isolate the electronic transfer. He felt that he might have to hire a friend of his, a computer hacker, who was a genius with a keyboard. The only problem was, the hacker was very expensive and he wanted his money up front. Jake was broke and Maxie was just plain tapped out. She'd begged Jake to try harder. The new nightclub was poised to open as soon as the license came through, which Dorrie thought would be any day now. Besides that, she missed her sister and longed to see her soon.

She wasn't going to acknowledge how much she missed Austin. She wondered what was taking him so long. Could he have given up? She tried to will away the sharp pang of disappointment the thought caused, then cursed herself for being such a fool. That's exactly what she needed him to do.

Yet, that would be hard for her to believe. Austin wasn't a quitter. He'd seemed determined to bring her back and get his money.

She pulled up in front of a Spanish-style house with a red tile roof. Mrs. Granger was sitting outside in her old rocker—a pastime that gave her great pleasure. She especially loved seeing the little boys and girls walking back and forth to school.

Maxie waved to the old woman as she removed the basket from its secure ties on the back seat. Feeling like Little Red Riding Hood going to Grandma's house, she swung the basket and wondered when that old Big Bad Wolf would show up.

The old woman rose when Maxie got to the porch. She hugged her tight. "Good to see you, my dear. What do you have for me today?"

"Hi, Mrs. Granger. I have Star's freshly made buttermilk biscuits along with her spicy salsa, just the way you like it. Handlebar tucked in a pound of your fancy coffee. Snake gave you a package of his favorite gumdrops. I'll let you look through the rest of the stuff and be surprised."

"What? No whiskey, dear?"

Maxie laughed. It was a joke between them when she'd begun to first bring the baskets. Everyone knew that Mrs. Granger never drank.

They sat for a while and when Sam Marks walked by with his dog, Mrs. Granger said, "Me and Sam used to date. Did you ever consider that men are like machinery, Maxie?"

"In what way, Mrs. Granger?" The old woman started rocking in her chair and Maxie followed suit.

"Well, take Raymond across the street." She gestured to the adobe house opposite them. "He's like a sports car."

"Huh?"

"You know, dear, fast and sleek." Mrs. Granger winked at Maxie and laughed out loud.

"Mrs. Granger," Maxie said, shock in her voice.

"Oh honey, I've been around the block. Consider Tom, who runs the grocery. I dated him in high school. He's like a helicopter." Mrs. Granger pantomimed whirling blades with her finger.

"A helicopter?"

"Lots of noise, very little movement."

Maxie sputtered with laughter. "And Sam?"

"He's the best of them all, a tugboat, slow and sure." Maxie turned and touched Mrs. Granger's arm and laughed at her shenanigans.

"Oh dear," Mrs. Granger said, "That one's a roller coaster."

Maxie's head whipped around and her eyes settled on two-hundred-and-fifteen pounds of gorgeous, tenacious Native American male.

Austin.

He smiled, but it wasn't like the beautiful, genuine one he'd given her in the motel room and a sharp pain nipped at her heart. His smile was purely evil, and disappointment shone in his eyes.

"Having a good time?" Austin said, putting his hands on his hips.

''How did you know I was here?''

''Star told me as nice as you please. She thinks it's very funny that I've been here twice to pick you up. She can't wait to hear about how you'll escape me a third time.''

''What took you so long?''

He stalked up to the porch and said to Mrs. Granger, ''Good evening, ma'am.'' He grabbed Maxie by the arm and prompted her to her feet.

''Oh, he looks like fun, Maxie.''

''Believe me. *Fun* isn't in Austin's vocabulary.''

With a muscle jerking in his jaw, he towed her from the porch to his car. ''Get in.''

''Aren't you going to search me?''

''The only place I want to put my hands right now is around your neck. Now let's go.''

She could see that Austin was getting angrier by the minute. She got in the car. When they passed the Lucky Star, Maxie protested. ''Austin, I need my stuff. I can't wear this all the way to Sedona.''

With a muttered curse, he whipped the car around and drove her to the bar in silence. It scared her how silent he was. She glanced over at him and saw the tenseness of his jaw.

''I'll go get my things.''

His voice stopped her. ''You know, on some level I understand why you did this. We have the same motivations. And I'm sorry you have to be the one the law is after. But I won't go back on a promise. You've just shown me that you won't either.''

"Austin. I didn't mean to let us get out of control. I...um...when you...kissed me...I..."

"Just get your stuff."

"I'm trying to explain."

"This is not a game. This is what I do for a living. I need this bounty."

Without warning, shame flashed over her like an uncontrollable flood. Before she could say a word, he interrupted. "Back at the hotel...how could you do that to me?"

"I'll get my things." More guilt and more shame. She was only being swamped with it. It wasn't until she went through the door of her room that she discovered he was right at her back.

The door slammed behind him, and she felt his hand on her arm. Turning her around, he leaned in close.

"When I kissed you. What? What did you feel? Triumph? Were you glad that I'd lost my control?"

"No."

His mouth came down on hers without warning, hot, demanding. She could feel the hurt in his kiss, the pain of her betrayal, and all she could feel was tenderness. He didn't harm her, as she knew he wouldn't. He was wounded and desperate to prove to himself that it meant nothing.

And she was just as desperate to prove to herself that he meant nothing to her.

"I woke up six hours later and it took me a day and a half to get my car fixed before I could track you down. You left me hard and aching. I'm still hard and aching and I can't help wanting you. But I don't trust you.''

"You don't have to, Austin. You want sex. We want sex.''

He shook his head. "It would be a mistake, another damn complication. More trouble.''

"Let me give you what you need.''

Beneath his shirt, she drew her nails against the sensitive skin of his lower stomach. Austin arched and cried out. He grabbed at her hands, but she whispered softly, "Let me.''

It was a struggle. She could see the hard-won struggle in his eyes. She drew her nails down his abdomen again and watched as his eyes closed and that look of rapture, almost pain, came over his face. He was beautiful to look at, beautiful in his surrender.

"Let me,'' she asked again, and kneaded the backs of her fingers against his rigid abdomen. He groaned deep in his chest and moved restlessly against her.

His hands moved around to hold her tightly against him. He closed his eyes, his voice husky. "I think we've moved beyond just sex, Maxie.''

She looked up at him and realized that he was right. Their relationship had progressed further than either one of them wanted to admit, but only Austin had had the courage to say what he felt.

Maxie could feel the coiled need in him as he strained to hold on to his self-control. She felt the quivers throughout his body as he tried to master his raging desire, and she felt him lose the battle with himself. He gripped her buttocks tighter and drove himself upward, grinding his hips against her stomach.

"Don't tell me that, Austin. It's too much to think about, and all I want is to hold you in my hands, take you into my mouth." She trembled while the delicious weakness flooded through her.

She unfastened the button of his jeans and searched for the zipper tab, sliding it down. She watched as the teeth separated and slowly exposed a widening V of tanned skin that gradually gave way to paler flesh. A dark swath of hair made a silky path down the hard muscles of his stomach and disappeared into the deeper shadows cast by his clothing. "No underwear. You are reckless, after all."

He was panting, and he made a grab for her, but she slipped down his body, pulling his jeans with her. The sexy fact that he didn't wear any underwear turned her on. His penis was long, thick and dark-skinned as it rose from the thatch of hair at his groin. "And you have nothing to be ashamed of." She stroked a fingertip over its blunt head.

His penis jerked up against the hard wall of his stomach at the touch. She wrapped her hand around it and lightly squeezed, amazed at the difference between the velvet-smooth surface and the delicious hardness beneath her hand.

6

AUSTIN SUCKED AIR. He reached for the hand she'd wrapped around his erection, intending to peel her fingers away and get control once again. Instead, he found himself wrapping his own hand over hers and directing it up and down his shaft for several strokes. Then squeezing his eyes shut against the sensations, he did what he should have done right away and removed both their hands.

But like quicksilver, her hands slipped out of his grasp. Just like *she* constantly slipped out of his grasp.

When she took him into her mouth, he jerked, staggering until his back was against the wall. He took in a sharp breath of air as her lips touched his silky head. Kissing him lightly, she moved slowly, as if she didn't want to rush any part of this. He couldn't let out his breath as she licked him in a circle, and then took the crown in her mouth. As she flicked her tongue, sucking hard at the same time, he finally let his breath go, sending an almost painful groan with it.

He said her name, soft and shaky. Gripping him with her hand, she pulled him into her mouth. Then with a steady rhythm that matched his heartbeat, she moved her tongue up and down the length of him. She pulled back, pausing to use the tip of her tongue, then moved down again as far as she could go.

Sensation after sensation played up and down his shaft, almost unbearable, almost painful. He could barely breathe at the soft, wet, movement of her mouth.

He fought against the hot, hard spiral of his orgasm. He gripped her arms and drew her away.

"No," she rasped out against his ear, against his grip on her wrist. She refused to be immobilized. "I need to...need to..."

Her soft mouth seared his lips and he couldn't think as his thoughts went spiraling out of control. Her hands cupped him again and moved up and down until he could no longer control his own body. He made a thick, guttural sound and thrust heavily against her hands, consumed her mouth, tunneled his fingers through her hair, and held her mouth against his.

Out of control.

He was way out of control.

He had to stop. Now. He knew it. Had to.

His thoughts went spiraling away into a frenzy of sensation and hot, tight, relentless hands. Her scent made him dizzy; the sight of her made him lust; the feel of her hands made him crazy.

His breathing was ragged, the sensations tight and sharp, and wouldn't be denied as he came hard, jack-knifing against her hands. His body was rigid as pleasure poured through him. His shaft pulsated hard as he cried out, her mouth a hot brand against his throat. Panting and moaning, his knees buckled and he sank to the floor, dragging Maxie with him.

She left him and he couldn't have stopped her even if he wanted to, even if she ran. But in minutes she was back. A hot, wet washcloth cleaned away his release and he closed his eyes at the tender way she washed him.

It was the second time in his life that he took. Greedily took. He opened his eyes and watched as she stroked his body slowly and lovingly. "Maxie." His voice came out husky.

She looked up and smiled. "What?"

He didn't know what to say. The words would not come. Instead, he reached out and drew her against him, kissing her mouth.

This was not the way he'd fantasized they would be—he would be. Well, not the first time, anyway. He'd wanted a quiet room with a wide bed and silk sheets with hours of exploration and discovery ahead of them. He wanted to bring her to the edge of ecstasy, ease back and take her there again, before finally tumbling with her into a pleasure-soaked darkness where he could saturate himself in the sweetness of her body. A lengthy, sweaty, shimmering, overwhelming, energy-sapping encounter that she would never forget.

He didn't want her to forget him.

He'd gotten his pleasure and it should have been enough, but he wanted more. He hadn't satisfied all the rampant sexual curiosity he was harboring about her. Though she'd slaked his lust, that should have been the end of it.

Her opinion of him meant more than just the physical. It suddenly, overwhelmingly meant everything to him. With that revelation, he realized that she was probably telling the truth about the money and clearing her name. He was supposed to be putting distance between them, but it seemed that every step he took brought her closer and closer to him—to his heart.

Burying his face in her short curls, he shivered. When she slipped her arms around him, cupping the back of his neck, feelings he didn't want to examine too closely overtook him, making him edgy.

He broke away from her, cursing her, cursing himself. The vision of her in jail rose in his mind. She'd be in a cold cell, all alone and shivering. He didn't like that vision and he didn't want to think about it. It was much easier to talk. Convince himself that he had to take her in.

"What were you doing sitting on that porch as if you didn't have a care in the world? You're not even trying to outrun me." He reached out and cupped her chin, bringing her eyes level with his.

"No. I don't need to outrun you." She met his gaze, her eyes a brilliant blue in the dim room.

"What?"

"I told you my story." She pulled her chin out of his fingers. Her soft skin cupped in his hand made his insides go crazy.

He shifted on the floor, bracing his back more

firmly against the wall. "You told me some sob story," he said, but he gentled his voice.

It didn't seem to matter to Maxie what tone he used. She bristled, her spine going ramrod straight. "It wasn't a sob story. It's the truth. I'm not going back to Sedona until I'm good and ready."

"I know it's the truth." The words came out of his mouth and surprised even him, but he was sure about what she'd said. Except there wasn't anything he could do about it.

"What did you just say?"

"I said I think you're telling the truth. I can't fault you for escaping—twice. But I can't let you go either." He turned his face away and rose to adjust his clothes, so she wouldn't see him wince at those words. "I'm still bringing you in."

"You can try. I'm ready to face the charges the moment I can clear my name."

She got up and grabbed a hold of one of his belt loops and jerked him close. His body was too ready to give in again to the hot temptation of her.

"You're not ditsy at all, but smart and sweet. I hope Jake works fast...." He swallowed hard when she ran her hand around and cupped his backside.

"I have to admit something to you, Austin. When you called me ditsy, it did make me want to show you up."

"That gives you pleasure?"

"A little satisfaction, yes."

He tilted his head and gave her a look full of skepticism.

"Okay. It gave me a lot of satisfaction."

"So it did give you pleasure to see me ass over tea kettle in that bathtub?"

"Pleasure? No. What gave me pleasure was watching your face when you came in my hands, feeling the hot, hard contours of your body, holding your rigid erection in my hands. That gave me a lot of pleasure. I bet you know just how to pleasure a woman. I bet you know many, many ways."

He groaned. The woman was going to kill him. Her hands moved up his body. "Austin, you are so beautiful." Her mouth reached up and he couldn't deny her anything as he claimed her hot mouth, her demanding lips. He wanted to sink into her hot wet heat with a need that was almost too big for him to manage.

He held her by her upper arms and backed her onto the bed, pushing his hips against her with a deep, all-consuming moan.

He could feel her clever hands on the snap of his jeans and, when she pulled the zipper down, sanity returned. He couldn't do this. Maxie had told him that she got satisfaction from besting him. This was just another ploy. But God, he cared about her and her sister. Damn them. He cared what happened to her club. He'd known it wouldn't take much to get him to feel close to her. He remembered her photograph. She was like a whirlwind, sucking everything into her, creating a vortex of need and want.

Her hundred-watt-smile, her sweet voice, her spontaneous personality, her killer body all pulled him in, but he had to resist. Jessica depended on him. Everyone in his family depended on him and this income. At this moment, Jessica's future could ride on the money he made off this bounty.

It tore him up inside to know that she was innocent and he couldn't do a thing about it. According to the rules he followed, her innocence wasn't his concern.

"Thanks for believing me."

He liked everything about Maxie, but he liked the sensual promise of her even more. Lessons in life were sometimes learned quickly, and at other times, not ever learned well enough. The lesson she taught him would stay with him forever. Honor and duty had to come before anything else, because it was the basis on which he'd built his life. He relished the teasing, the sharpened awareness, but he also realized that nothing could come of it. It was hard to admit that he enjoyed just the expectation with her ten times beyond what he felt during the act with any other woman. He wondered if it would fade with time and then realized he would never know.

The smartest way to handle Francesca Maxwell was to do his job and clear out of her life. And he couldn't do that until he got to Sedona.

He pulled away from her as a knock sounded on the door. Austin rose and did up his pants. Maxie walked to the door and opened it. Star stood there.

She glanced at Austin, and when she realized what he was doing, a gleam came into her eye. "I see that he found you."

"Yes, he did," Maxie said, meeting the woman's knowing gaze straight on.

"Couldn't have been too hard. I told him exactly where you'd be. Of course, catching you isn't really his problem, is it?" She laughed. "See you next time around, Maxie." She leaned in and gave Austin a cheeky grin. "Until next time, bounty boy."

He grabbed Maxie's hand, snatched her makeshift bag of things and brushed past a smug Star. "Wait. I need my purple bag. I have something important in…"

"Tough. We're leaving." He wanted to save her. He did, but he'd taken an oath and how could he face himself in the mirror if he didn't do his job. Except now, doing the right thing wasn't feeling so right to him. He admired what Maxie was trying, but it didn't change the facts. He was trapped and so was she.

WHEN THEY PULLED into Cimarron hours later, he took her with him when he checked into the room. Maxie wasn't sure what that meant or whether it meant anything at all. He asked her if she was hungry and they found an all-night diner. He was edgy as they ate, but when the door closed behind them at the hotel, he seemed to get more agitated and jumpy. He was afraid of anymore contact with her of either a physical or emotional nature.

She sensed his withdrawal and did everything she could not to touch him.

After he snapped the handcuffs first to his wrist and

then to hers, he turned out the lights. The darkness was very thick and almost oppressive.

On a soft whisper, she touched his mouth. "I scare you, don't I?"

"You scare me? Yes, dammit, you do. I don't like this situation. It should be cut and dried and it's way too complicated," he confessed.

"And you don't like complications, do you?" Maxie asked, sucking in her breath when he slid his hand down her neck, his thumb absently stroking her throat.

She closed her eyes at the distracting feel of his caress.

"No. I like to have control. I feel off-balance without it. Bounty hunting is supposed to be clear-cut. Pick up the skip and collect a paycheck. This gnaws at me because I care about what happens to you and to your sister."

"My situation makes you have to change your way of thinking."

"Yes," he admitted softly. "I feel like change is coming, and I'm not prepared for it. I don't like change."

"What kind of change are we talking about here?" she questioned. Sliding her free arm around him, she pulled him into a loose, almost friendly embrace. But her thoughts were far from friendly and she gasped softly when his chest pressed against hers.

"The kind of change that's irrevocable. My life. Your life. The kind that breaks foundations and hearts."

"Ah, violent change." She nodded her head and shivered.

"Then what I guess we have to decide is simply, is it worth it?" She flattened herself against him, and her eyes widened when she felt the hard heat of him press against her. "Austin…" She would have to take this time with him and treasure it. Her feelings were stronger than she'd realized, and her heart was at risk. But the risk was worth it. She knew it in her soul.

"Shh," he murmured, pressing his finger over her lips. "Just let me hold you." By now her eyes had adjusted to the dark. He watched her, his eyes smoky and intent, his expression taut. A fluttery weakness moved through her, and it took all the willpower she had to keep from giving into the drugging sensation. She couldn't let herself get lost in it this time.

Feeling as if every nerve in her body was stretched to the limit, she avoided his gaze, but Austin cupped her face and brought it back up to his hungry eyes.

Overwhelmed by his action, she turned her face into his hand. Austin inhaled sharply and cupped the back of her neck. Murmuring her name, he drew her into his arms and covered her mouth in a kiss that heated her blood, and touched her heart.

Austin stopped kissing her and with a heart-wrenching look in his eyes he stared at her as if she was shining gold. He closed his eyes, his mouth sought hers in a sudden need that passed from him into her. She parted her lips as she hung on to him. She pushed her hips between his thighs and tight to his groin. The feel of his hard male body, fully aroused, made her moan softly into his frantic mouth.

Austin shifted his hold on her back, and resealed his hot, hungry lips against hers in a kiss that seemed to ravage her very soul. A kiss that was fueled by loneliness, by need, by a fever of want. It went on and on until Maxie was swimming in a sea of desire.

"Austin," she pleaded, knowing that she was asking for his touch and not being able to deny herself the pleasure.

"Maxie, you don't know what you're asking," he said, the surrender already in his voice.

"Yes," she panted. "Yes, I do. Oh God, please Austin."

"I don't have any protection."

"If only you'd let me get my purple bag. There were condoms in there."

As if realizing that she was beyond recovery, Austin released her and got the key, and removed the cuffs. He twisted her against one thigh and shifted his hold. Tightening his arm around her torso, he slid his hand over her buttocks until he reached the buttons of her shorts. Slowly he opened them and she could feel the provocative heat of his hand against the heart of her. His fingers caught the waistband of her shorts and suddenly he was absorbing her cry as he touched her where she so wanted to be touched. Maxie clutched at him, her body going taut, and he pressed her face into the curve of his neck as she automatically bowed against the caressing heat of his fingers. An explosion ignited inside her, and a series of convulsions ripped through her as she came apart in his arms. Austin hugged her against him, his arm supporting her back.

Unable to speak, Maxie cried his name against his neck, and removing his hand from her shorts, he enfolded her in a powerful, all-encompassing embrace.

She tried to move off him and his voice was strained when he whispered against her temple. "Don't."

Maxie tightened her arms around him, too spent to make a reply, knowing it was going to hurt when she had to trick him again.

MAXIE DREAMED. Erotic, sensual dreams of Austin, his hard hands, his taut body, his beautiful mouth. She moaned and shifted, but always resettled. There was a warmth that surrounded her, cocooned her with a strong presence that made her feel safe and secure. Something tickled her nose, and her eyelids fluttered. A wonderful heady scent filled her nostrils. She found herself trying to identify that scent. She reached up to brush away that aggravating tickle. She froze when her hand moved over a stubbled cheek. Then her fingers slid into thick hair, and that wonderful scent registered on her brain and brought her to full awareness. He was a devastating man to wake up to.

Austin was still asleep, his black lashes thick on his amazing cheekbones. When he was awake she barely noticed them because of his intense eyes.

Unable to stop her exploration, she trailed her hand down the strong column of his throat. He shifted and exhaled but didn't wake. Emboldened, she let her fingertips glide over the heavy, velvet muscles of his chest, over the hard, ridged muscle of his abdomen down to the waistband of his jeans.

No underwear. It would be so easy to release him. With a flick of her wrist and slide of a zipper, she could have him hard and hot in her hands. She could have him moaning and crying out like he had in her little room behind the bar in Mesa Roja. She wanted the quick, uncontrollable thrust of his hips, sliding hot powerful flesh between her hands, making her heart pound, her body throb.

A strong hand gripped her wrist and her head whipped around to find Austin fully awake.

7

AUSTIN CLENCHED his jaw when her hand settled at the snap to his jeans. Her touch created a focal point of heat beneath his flesh. He bit back on the lust that crawled edgily into his belly. This wasn't good timing. He was hard and hot already from thinking about her. It wouldn't take much to slide her beneath him and slake his hunger.

But they had no protection, and he wasn't going to risk it. It was the first time in his life he didn't curse his formidable control. He needed it now, desperately.

He'd never wanted a woman more than he wanted Maxie. A sudden realization had his hand curling against the steel of the handcuff. As much as he wanted her physically, he wanted the woman more. Wanted to look into her eyes and see only himself reflected there. Wanted the right to press his hand to the small of her back. Wanted… Mentally, he hesitated. Was he falling in love with her? Had he already fallen?

The questions brought a rush of emotion he wasn't quite sure how to handle. If the answers were there, he couldn't see them, or maybe he wasn't ready to see them.

"There's no protection."

Her shoulders slumped and she leaned back into him, making his breath hitch at the feel of her soft skin against his.

"Right. I forgot."

"It's easy to forget, but the consequences would be hard to forget."

He reached down and got the key and unlocked the cuffs. He eased away from her. "I have to say that I'm at a loss as to what to do." He didn't have any second thoughts about his growing feelings for her. His heart had tightened painfully when she so trustingly slid into his arms last night. If he were to make love to her, he was afraid he would lose a part of himself, probably for good.

She met his gaze candidly. "I'm not going to say I don't want to sleep with you, Austin, because I do. Take it for what it's worth."

"Right. You don't mind hot, wild sex."

"Sex with you and escaping you are two different things. I can separate the two."

"I have a hard time doing that. It's not very honorable on my part to be sleeping with a person I'm taking in so I can collect money on her. It's a bizarre situation."

"I agree with you, but I don't like the alternative. Once I get back to Sedona there isn't going to be any time. We only have this. Right now."

"Maxie, it's not that easy."

"It is that easy." They stared at each other for a long moment. "Your honor is one of the things I admire in you. I'll get my stuff together. I'm sure you want to get on the road. You have a bounty to collect.''

"That's right," he said with resignation. "I do."

When she disappeared into the bathroom, the words rang in his head like a bell. *You have a bounty to collect.*

His sister was depending on him. How could he have forgotten that? Easy. He wanted Maxie and not for a few nights and days. A part of him wanted to go after her with everything he had. Another part of him—the part that told him that this situation was too complicated—couldn't accept that she was going to jail and he was the man who was going to put her back there.

That part of him sent the message to get the job done, to not want. To beware.

Still, that same part of him didn't know what the hell to do with her.

IT WAS NOON when they drove into Taos about three and one half hours away from Albuquerque and another eight hours to Sedona. Maxie immediately liked the narrow dusty streets. She noticed the interesting men and women who walked the streets as if they had gotten caught in some kind of time warp. The people of Taos looked like they hadn't wanted to give up their hippie days.

Yet the numerous art galleries caught her eye and she wished she had a chance to visit them. The town's adobe structures were also distinct landmarks of the southwest.

Although the town was interesting, the scenery was breathtaking. There was the high desert mesa, broken in two by the six-hundred and fifty foot chasm of the Rio Grande. Wheeler's Peak, New Mexico's tallest crest, was situated in the impressive Sangre de Cristo Mountain range. Taos was a feast for the eyes from the forested uplands to the sage-carpeted mesa.

When Austin pulled over into the parking lot of an inn set around a courtyard marked by an eighty-foot-long portal, surrounded by pine and fruit trees, Maxie said, ''Austin, what are you doing?''

He didn't look at her, his hands tight on the wheel. She reached out. He turned and pulled her into an embrace, kissing her mouth with a longing she felt all the way to her heart.

When he broke the kiss, he looked down at her. ''I thought about what you said. You're right. All we have is now. We could stay here, at least a little while?''

She reached up and cupped his face, her insides turning to mush. ''Yes. I'd love to.''

He opened the passenger side door, and helped Maxie out of the car. She asked, ''Can I come in with you, to check in? It's too hot out here to wait.''

He just looked down into her face as if he was immune to her charms, but Maxie knew better. She could feel his heart beating hard against the tough wall of his chest. ''I'm not cuffing you to the steering wheel anymore.''

He took off her handcuffs. "I can't let you go, but I...can't treat you like that anymore."

She was supposed to be keeping him off his guard, but she was the one losing her focus. This new, sweeter Austin might make it easier for her to escape, but the same sense of guilt surfaced at the thought of duping him now. "Don't tell me you're loosening up a little," she teased.

He smiled and Maxie took a quick intake of breath. She should care more about getting away, but she couldn't concentrate on that right now.

"Don't tell the other bounty hunters, it'll ruin my reputation."

She laughed and his smile widened. "Austin, you have a sense of humor. I'm stunned. I could have sworn you'd had it removed."

"Lady," he growled. "I do have a sense of humor or I'd be in the loony bin right now with all this traveling back and forth."

Maxie took advantage of the closeness and his sparkling eyes to study him. The feeling that he was two different men struck her once again. There was a hard edge to him, and don't-touch-me-I-bite signs bristling all around him. But that soft look that sometimes came over his face drove her crazy, and made her want to goad him until he revealed what she'd only glimpsed.

He stepped away from her. "Let's get inside."

"If you ask me, we just keep walking toward the fire."

He gave her a startled glance, but chose to keep on walking.

AFTER CHECKING IN and getting the room key, they returned to the car. Austin opened the door and extracted their belongings.

They walked over to the inn and found their room. He handed Maxie the key and she opened the door, then closed it after they'd entered.

She surveyed the room. "Now we're talking." The room was sumptuously decorated. The walls had hand prints and petroglyph motifs, and a comfortable couch along with a fireplace. She walked into the bathroom and said, "Austin, they have a jet tub in here with bubble bath and candles."

She returned, unzipped her bag and pulled out a clean shirt. She turned her back to Austin and stripped off both the shirt she was wearing and the silk camisole underneath, dropping both garments on the bed. She quickly donned the other shirt, but she could feel his eyes boring into her back.

She hungered for more than his body and that, she knew without a doubt was probably the most dangerous thing she'd ever wanted. It jeopardized her plan to get away from him and be true to her sister and their plans, which were blowing away as quickly as the sands of the desert. Making love with Austin wouldn't be a good idea. Giving him her heart would be even more stupid. Yet, she felt one was inevitable and the other—well, the other one she didn't want to think about.

If she got any closer to him, she would find it much harder to carry out her plans, but on the other hand, she didn't want to waste this small, precious time with him. How would she find the strength to escape him again if her heart softened any more towards him and his family? If she could convince him to let her go, it would be easier on both of them. And if Jake got the evidence, she would be home free.

He walked up to her and grabbed her upper arm. "You are the most immodest woman I know."

She jumped, his touch setting off firecrackers in her blood. She was reeling from the thought that she was losing her heart. No way was she close to falling in love with him. Was she?

She couldn't be, she told herself as she looked up into his face. *Please no.*

"Why couldn't you have stayed that guy?"

"What guy?"

"The guy that believed if he couldn't fight it or handcuff it, he was stumped. Why did you have to change?"

"You don't want to stay here with me? I thought this would give me time...give us time to...I don't know. Just more time."

She wanted to scream, even as she breathed a sigh of relief. She turned away from him and headed for the door. Suddenly, she felt too confined and edgy, feelings she didn't like. It took Austin a moment to catch up with her.

"Where do you think you're going?"

"I need to walk. I'm antsy. Do you mind?"

AUSTIN SIGHED and fell into step with her. She felt as if they'd left more than just the hotel behind. Maxie looked up at the sky. "I wish it would rain."

"You're in luck. It may look dry and sunny here, but afternoon thunderstorms are common."

"Rain in the desert always seems so exotic."

"Why?"

"Because it rarely rains there. When it does, it seems otherworldly, amazing..."

"Impossible. Yeah, like what's between us."

"It's nothing but hormones between us, Austin."

"Who are you trying to convince? Me or you?"

"It's the situation, the danger, heightened senses. If we were ever to get into a regular relationship we would probably be bored out of our skulls." Maybe if she said this over and over she would believe it.

"It's true that nothing about all this is regular, but I doubt that I'd be bored with you."

"Believe me."

"Especially if I was the guy to turn you over to the law."

"Then don't do it. Just let me go." Slowly, her gaze rose to his.

"*Let go.* Easy words, Maxie. Two simple, little words."

"But they're not easy for you." She touched his forearm, curling her fingers around his heat.

"No."

"Because you take your job seriously."

"Yes, I take my job seriously."

"Of course you do. I'm not saying that you don't. It's a bizarre situation, like you said. I'm innocent of all the charges and you believe me."

"That's all true, but it's not really the point. My job is to track you down and bring you in. I'm not a judge or a lawyer or even law enforcement. I'm just a bounty hunter and my part in your situation is straightforward."

"Would it be hard for you to look the other way?"

"Yes. It would."

"So you want what with me here?"

"Time, Maxie. I wish I could put it into better words, but I know that you'll hate me when I turn you in and I just want time."

"Sex? Do you want that too?"

"I want what you're willing to give. That's all. I can't explain why I stopped, even to myself. It seemed like everything was getting out of control." He reached down and picked up her hands. "Look at your wrists. It kills me to put those cuffs on you now, seeing what they're doing to your skin. I can't imagine what it's doing to you on the inside. Bringing you in seems wrong to me, but I have no choice in the matter. I took an oath."

She clasped her hands around his wrists. He might tell her he wanted time with her. He might say that her situation was hard, but he was also saying that he was honor-bound and on a quest, somewhat like the knights of old. "Duty is important to you. You showed it to me by your dedication to your family. The moment they needed you, you dropped everything, your dreams and hopes. You supported them without strings attached. I can't fault you. That's my dilemma. That's how I feel inside. I just can't fault you."

The truth of the matter was that the time he wanted would give her the time to find a way out of this mess. She could escape from him the moment his guard was down. She would play along. It wouldn't be hard at all to pretend to care for him. But her priorities hadn't changed. She wasn't going back to Sedona. Not for him, not for anyone.

The thoughts hurt, but she refused to consider why. Instead she assured herself that she and Austin were adults. They were completely capable of appeasing their physical needs without becoming tangled in a snare.

He grabbed her arm, making her stop in mid stride. "Where do we go from here?"

Maxie shrugged. She so wanted to say nowhere. They were at an impasse. "Let's just walk."

"All right."

She slipped her arm through his and continued walking, trying to ignore the feel of his hand on her skin, the intense look in his eyes. He would be wild in bed, out of control. She knew it. She'd already held him in her hands.

She closed her eyes briefly. He would be magnificent.

The sudden sound of gushing water made Maxie glance at Austin, then at the sky, but there was no rain, although clouds were gathered thick and menacing. As Maxie turned the corner with Austin right at her heels, she saw the source of the water.

Some neighborhood kids had turned on a hydrant. They were cavorting in the stream that plumed straight up to feed the thirsty asphalt of the street, raining big fat droplets on the foliage of the sheltering park just behind the hydrant. The sign in front read Kit Carson Park.

Someone flipped on a boom box and sultry salsa music burst into the gloom of the afternoon. Doors opened and people began to emerge and dance beneath the water.

Maxie took Austin's hand and headed toward the water, but he held back. She finally let go and went into the spray alone.

The music fired her blood as she danced with the others, kicking up water, twirling around and shouting with laughter into the night.

Austin watched her as he squatted on his haunches, using a palm tree for support while an edgy, gripping need churned inside him. He had tried to resist her charm. She wanted nothing more than to escape him and she would use anything to do it, including her tantalizing femininity. Why had he stopped in Taos? He was at a loss to understand it himself. He had no intention of giving in to her request to let her go. This act of insanity had seemed like such a good idea when he'd pulled over and it was true what he'd said. He wanted time, but it would only serve to make what he had to do harder. He was willing to embrace that. It was already worthwhile as he watched her move in the dusky, surreal afternoon. Not ditsy, not stupid, as he would liked to have believed, but a beautiful woman who loved to sing, dance and laugh.

A sudden savage need overcame him, swirling through him with a devastating effect. Her high, firm breasts were exposed through the white shirt she wore, her nipples tight and puckered and his mouth ached to taste her skin. The untamed craving intensified as his eyes traveled down her exquisite body, lingering on her hips as they swayed to the now soft and sultry music.

Maxie ran her hands through her wet hair, slicking it back. Suddenly, she felt a thrill of apprehension brush her skin. She turned her head slightly and found Austin's dark eyes staring at her. She had never seen such a wild look in his eyes. *Wild in bed.* That thought surfaced with a rush of passion so intense that Maxie had to bite her lip.

The velvet depths burned with such powerful desire that she shivered, held immobile by his heavy-lidded gaze. Fiery heat began to build in the pit of her stomach. Although he lounged against the tree, she could see the tautness of his muscles as he suddenly pushed away, the muscles of his chest thick and rippling with the movement. When he rose in such a beautiful flowing motion, she was reminded of a rising tiger. She watched in wonder as he started toward her, the movement of the corded muscles of his thighs holding her attention like a fine piece of art. Magnificently he stalked in her direction as if she were prey. His dark eyes never left her face. She couldn't have moved even if she had been threatened, so captivated was she by the primitive need she sensed in his body. The need was intensified and abundantly answered by her own body, her skin prickling with a sudden wild desire she saw mirrored in his eyes.

As he moved into the stream of the water, everything about him seemed to deepen and intensify as if an ephemeral light glowed from within. The blackness of his hair got blacker, the blue of his jeans a deeper, mesmerizing blue, the white of his T-shirt starker in the night. He reached her. Stretching out one steely hand, he caught her wrist and drew her into the alluring realm of his powerful embrace. His hands slid slowly, sensuously, down her back, pulling her hips against his, so she could feel the hard heat of the desire that flared inside him. She quivered violently at the shock, involuntarily bucking against him, only to find herself further electrified by the closeness of his face.

Her arms went around his neck, the sultry music moving both of them in the suddenly hushed night. Her heart beat hard when he stepped away from her and slid his hands down her arms to her hands. He tugged and drew her into the sheltering trees and dense foliage of the park. Once inside its dim lush interior, he drew her against his body.

''How I want you,'' he said against the sensitive shell of her ear, sending a multitude of chills down her back. He thrust his hands into her wet hair, almost savagely, clenching the thick, spiky strands between his fingers, easing her head back, tilting her face up to his. With a low growl of animal lust, his mouth descended to her waiting lips as he fervently kissed her over and over, until her mouth was on fire from his burning lips.

"She was right."

"Who," he rasped against her lips.

"That nice old lady in Mesa Roja, Mrs. Granger. She said you were a roller coaster."

"What's that supposed to mean?"

"You know when you ride a roller coaster how you get that breathless anticipation when you're climbing to the pinnacle and then you drop suddenly."

"Yeah."

"I bet that's the way you make love, Austin, a breathless, sudden sense of falling."

"You want to find out, Maxie?" he said with such crushing need inherent in his voice that her name rang with his possession.

She could hear the word *mine* threaded into and around the sound of her name. Taking what he believed was his, knowing that he would not be denied. It was true, she was his. She'd been his from the moment they'd met. "Yes, I do."

With his mouth locked to hers, his hips moving rhythmically in his fevered passion, he demanded her response, commanded her to reply. Her lips were soft and yielding. He searched out every hidden place within, leaving no part of its dark moist cavity unexplored, unclaimed. Her head spun as he continued his fevered onslaught upon her senses. Her nostrils were full with the musky scent of his powerful body moving against hers. Her blood pumped strongly through her veins, her ears hearing the sweet music of his uncontrollable groans, her hands moving over the thick, pronounced muscles of his shoulders and back, kneading him. She was his woman—body, heart, and soul, aching with a need only he could fulfill.

He clutched for the hem of her shirt, raising it, releasing her breasts to his plundering mouth. She exulted in her own feminine power to get him to respond to her in such an obsessed and overwhelming way. She reveled in her ability to enthrall him, cage the restless, growling tiger inside of him, to hold him as much a prisoner as she.

With the suddenness of storms in the desert, thunder rolled overhead. It was as if he were part of the powerful storm rolling in untamed uncontrolled passion. Lightning flashed overhead, followed closely by a loud crash of thunder. The heavens spilt and a deluge poured from the skies, pelting their bodies with the warm, cooling water. She gasped at the sultry sensation of the plummeting drops of water against her breasts, as well as his warm, hot mouth, encompassing the tip of one breast, then the other. His tongue teased the rosy crests into stiff hard peaks that trembled and quaked with each intimate touch of his velvet lips. Rapturous tremors coursed through her body as moans of pleasure escaped her lips at the sweet sensations, hungering for more. Her hands came up against each side of his head, pulling his mouth closer to her, arching her back in wanton abandon as the storm raged overhead and inside of her.

Thunder boomed overhead with such a loud crash that it reverberated through her body. She gasped in one long moan of ecstasy as he slipped his hands between her clothing and her flesh, driving his finger into her so suddenly and deeply that it took her breath away. She inhaled sharply, raggedly, her breath catching on a pleasured groan. She heard him sigh, his gasp of pleasure at being inside her, even as he aroused them both to a feverish pitch by deliberately, tantalizingly withdrawing, then swiftly entering her again. His breath was hot against her throat and upon her breasts as his mouth devoured her, sucking her nipples greedily and laving them with his tongue. Frantically she arched against him as he moved against her.

The storm built, raging and churning into a turbulent fury. Her mind reeled with the pleasure as he rhythmically pressed against her desire-swollen nub. Her hips arched and bucked, wringing unrestrained cries from her until the pleasure was too much, too intense and it released in her with explosive force. She tangled her fingers in the black silk of his hair as she came powerfully around his fingers.

The loud, piercing sound of a siren split the air and Austin froze. He lifted his head and looked at her, quickly adjusting her clothing when he heard the cops break up the spontaneous party, urging people home and shutting off the hydrant.

His dark eyes came back to hers and closed. With a soft sigh, he slipped down her body to his knees. Maxie quickly tucked in her shirt and felt her heart breaking. She'd driven him to wanting her, knowing that he would fight against it, and she felt shame for it because she'd pushed him to the edge and all it would take was a small shove to send him over, but she thought, as she too closed her eyes, she wanted to soar with him.

She fixed her clothes and bent down, too. She cupped his face and looked into his eyes and saw everything that had been missing from her life, everything it could be, everything it should be.

He nodded and stood.

It took very little time to pick up what they needed.

AUSTIN WAS SUBDUED and quiet when they entered the hotel room. Maxie hovered near him, but seemed to be afraid of touching him. He didn't blame her. She should be scared. He was on the very edge of his control and he wasn't sure about this. Did she plan to trick him again in some way when he was lost in her? He needed time to regain equilibrium before he touched her. "Give me a minute," he said when she lifted her hand to touch him. He walked to the bed.

Suddenly his clinging, wet T-shirt was uncomfortable. Feeling confined and edgy, he pulled the shirt over his head and dropped it onto the floor. Then he glanced down.

It was the most mundane thing. His sodden T-shirt and her silky undergarment were entwined together on the floor at the foot of the bed. He reached down to pick up his shirt, but his hands touched the soft, silky material instead. He gasped, bringing the wispy garment up so he could take a better look at it. He stroked his hand against the sheer material, becoming aroused that Maxie had worn this cloth against her skin. He brought it to his nose, breathing deeply of her delicate fragrance. He closed his eyes at the powerful need that rocked through him. The material felt cool and silky against the bare skin of his chest. He rubbed the garment along his cheekbone almost groaning with pleasure.

His eyes opened and Maxie felt as if a blast furnace had suddenly materialized in the room such was the scorching flame she saw in his hot honey eyes, full of flickering flashes like caramel lightning. That gaze sent warmth tingling down her spine. One look from his sultry eyes could do this to her body—make it catch on fire and burn.

"Come here." His voice wavered unevenly.

She walked across the room as if under a spell. She could see the rock-hard need in him; he was almost tense with it.

When she reached him, he let the material slip out of his hands. It slid sensually down his chest, dropping in a whisper of sound to the floor.

She looked up into his desire-hardened face and felt compelled to touch him. She was overwhelmed that he needed her so much and knew it was not just sex. If it were, he wouldn't be so worried about where it would lead them. He would have taken her a long time ago without thought or protection. But she meant more to him than some bounty. She knew it in her soul and her heart contracted painfully knowing that there wasn't a thing she could do about his pain or her own. They would both just have to endure it, because what was between them was much more powerful than duty and honor. More powerful than liquor licenses and clearing her name. More powerful than anything.

Forced by her blatant need to reach out, she touched the hot sleek skin of his chest. He jerked, groaning and twisting his head to the side. Enthralled with his response, she trailed her hand down the middle of his chest over the banded muscles of his flat stomach. He groaned louder, his breathing rapid and harsh. She moved closer to him. "We are in trouble," she whispered, her voice coming out husky and strained with the riotous desire clamoring inside her.

"Maxie." His voice was tension filled, her name on his lips desire soaked.

She knew that was all he could manage, so caught up in his need for her he couldn't even speak. It was awesome to have a man want her so badly that he couldn't speak.

"We're crazy." She ran her hands farther down, slipping beneath the waistband of his jeans. His hands clutched her shoulders as if he were going to collapse, pushing the hard heat of his erection against her hand, burying his face into the hollow of her shoulder. She felt the power in his big hands on her shoulders. But he would never hurt her. That thought was like a rush of adrenaline to her bloodstream. She drew her nails up the tautly rigid shaft.

It was as if he couldn't move, couldn't think, he

could only let her do with him what she wanted. The pleasure that exploded inside of him sent his face deeper into the hollow. He panted open mouthed against her skin murmuring unintelligible words. She grasped the waistband of his jeans, peeled the offending garment away from his body, freeing the glorious burning weight of his shaft. She swiftly removed her clothing. And when her hands were free, she ran both palms across his hips and up his sides. With her full weight, she pushed him backward onto the bed. She raised her leg, dragging it up his stiff arousal, relishing the power she had over him when his head thrashed and he groaned deeply in his chest.

The pleasure of sliding along his thick, hard erection spiraled inside her.

Austin jerked and tried to rise.

Maxie deliberated for a moment, then asked, "Don't you want to cuff me to the bed? I won't be able to get away."

"Are you sure about this, Maxie?"

"Yes." The thought of being bound made the thrill inside her intensify, bound by a man she so desperately wanted to touch. It would intensify her pleasure, heighten it to be unable to use her hands.

He reached for the handcuffs and switched their positions. Pulling her arms over her head to close the cuffs around her wrists and around the slat in the bed.

He gently guided her chin up, tilted her head back as he lowered his. "You're safe," he murmured. "Safe with me."

The heat of his mouth was rivaled only by the softness of his lips. "Safe," he murmured against her mouth. The word a soft, charged promise. All thoughts flew out of her head in the sizzling aftermath of his kiss.

As if she was the only woman who could give him what he craved, he explored the sweet nectar of her mouth. His seductive tongue was like moist velvet. Maxie took from him as if he was the only man who could give her what she needed.

His fingers were deliberate, relentless and methodical as he stroked the skin around her breast. He touched her everywhere but the taut peak that craved his mouth. The mouth that conquered hers, branded her his. His caresses were too light, glided over skin sensitized by desire long denied. Aching for fulfillment that was only just a whisper away, she strove to hang on to each new sensation. His fingers promised, his mouth pledged that soon he would give her harder contact, the wet heat of his mouth, but the torturous caresses continued, leaving her arching and gasping.

He was aware of every sound she made as she uttered it, each time she shuddered. He brought her to the very edge of her endurance and beyond.

He drew his tongue up the globe of her breast. She could feel his hot breath hovering almost within reach of her straining nipple. With a fleeting flick with his tongue, he drew away and laved her other breast in the same manner until she was writhing beneath him. When his hot, searing mouth finally closed over her breast, sucking hard, Maxie went mad.

With a strangled moan she came up off the bed;

her hands fought the cuffs, wanting, needing to clench tightly into his hair, to feel the straining muscles of his back. Her body writhed beneath his, something she couldn't ever remember doing before.

"Austin, please." She wrapped her legs around his waist until she was flush against his hardness. Austin groaned and she loved the sound. Didn't think she could hear it enough. "Please."

"I want you so much it hurts." His mouth against the shell of her ear was tender, soothing.

"Please, Austin."

"But not reckless. Not fast." His voice was a whisper, feathering hot kisses against the skin between her breasts.

He was taking her to a new place, a place she was afraid she didn't want to reach, but he gave her no choice. She tried to press her enflamed flesh against the hot, sleek muscle of his hard body. She couldn't stand it. "Now. I want you inside me *now*."

"No."

She moaned in protest when he wouldn't comply with her demand. She fought the cuffs, pulling against them in her need to feel him inside her. But to no avail. Austin would have his way and she was powerless to do anything about it. All her thoughts burned up like fodder to flame with each swell of intense pleasure, each kiss he nibbled over her hot flesh. When he traced his tongue skillfully through the valley between her breasts, she stopped fighting the escalating sensation and surrendered.

He savored her.

His arms around her kept her grounded even as he took and gave, touched her, coerced her, tormenting, but satisfying. He was caught in the same tormenting need, his strategy backfiring to engulf him in the same flames that burned her.

With each stroke of his hand, the tension within her mounted. With each gasp and moan from her, his breath got harsher, hotter, more deliberate. He used his amazing control to drive her higher. He wanted to give her this because their time was so short. This was his way of leaving her with more than she had when she met him. Something that would linger long after they were separated. Even in her wildness, Maxie cherished it, knew it, accepted it.

His mouth lingered over her body as if she were a tasty feast and every flavor was exquisite, each ripe, rich. When he flattened his hand low on her belly, but not low enough to satisfy her, she was scorched. When he took a nipple in his mouth and bit down gently, she was consumed.

In a gruff, uneven voice he whispered her name across her lips, moving his mouth over hers with unrestrained longing. Thrusting his tongue in her mouth, she arched against him sobbing with desperation and need. When she felt his naked, hot shaft against her, she thrust her hips in an uncontrollable dance of passion.

"Look at me," he demanded and she did, but she couldn't stop moving against him. It was too much. But his eyes compelled her attention and mesmerized her. She couldn't look away.

It was there again, that shimmering passion she'd almost experienced in the hotel room in Albuquerque. She wanted to know it, wanted it to consume her, wanted him to make her his. He grabbed her hips, holding her still against him. "Wait." He took a ragged breath. "Just a minute."

It was an order, a plea, a prayer.

It took all her willpower to still her body. The cuffs clanged against the headboard and he looked at them and then down at her. With an incoherent sound he ran his hands up her body, around the curve of each breast. Hungry for him, Maxie could barely contain the power building in her muscles. When he groaned and grabbed what was on the bedside table, she smiled.

Her smile was replaced by a gasp of anticipation when he fitted the condom to himself, then lifted her hips to place a pillow under her, spread her thighs, and sluiced his hands down her legs, beginning with her inner thighs.

A killing pleasure speared through her, piercing and devastatingly fierce.

A pleasure to die for, to live for.

He splayed a hand down on her belly and fitted himself to her.

She accepted him with a startled moan of sheer pleasure arching her body off the bed to accept his deep frenzied drive, understanding all too well what drove him. The wildness that was a part of him, she knew, was unleashed, and as he powered into her, she welcomed the hard hot heat of delicious rapture.

Maxie lost her hold on reality as the sensations inside her started to gather and gather, pulling into one hot, pulsating center. He moved again and again and the sensations brought an agonized groan from her. He touched her, lifted her, brought her to the peak and held her back. Over and over.

Breaking down her barriers, then shoring them up.

She met every thrust of his body with hers, until she could bear it no longer. He pressed against her, wrapped his arms around her, buried himself as deeply inside her as he could, and sent her spiraling into that place where darkness and stars meld and ecstasy lives.

Her climax was long and convulsive, draining and glorious. She laughed and wept into it, tried to reach out to hold him, but the cuffs got in the way, held her back. Her body went slack and limp around him.

His thick shaft was hard, pulsating inside her.

When she could function, she opened her eyes to look at him. "Austin?"

He grinned and rocked his hips gently, eliciting an incoherent moan from her.

"Oh God."

"We're not done." He pulled out of her and unlocked one of the cuffs, then locked one to his wrist. He lifted her knees, wrapped them about his hips and entered her with one quick thrust, rolling with her clasped tightly to him.

"Ride me, Maxie."

She grabbed his free wrist and drew his arm over his head along with the cuffed one. Bracing herself on his hands, she leaned down and seared his lips with a hot, desperate kiss, loving the soft groan as she rolled her hips.

Then she rode him with slow, measured thrusts. He gasped and his body jackknifed in an uncontrollable movement of muscle and bone.

A violent tremor coursed through her, blinding her with desire. She clutched at him, a shock of sensation compelling her deeper and deeper, tempering her body with the steel of his own.

Austin moved his free hand, reached between their driving bodies and touched her. Her eyes widened and a ragged gust of air escaped her chest in a rush as that small, private contact sent her hurtling to the most splintering orgasm of her life.

Austin didn't take his eyes off her face. It was all the torture she guessed he could endure as he pumped his hips in uncontrollable thrusts, spilling his hot seed inside her.

8

"YOU KNOW I wouldn't mind staying handcuffed to you and in this bed until Jake calls and tells me my name is cleared. Then you won't have to chase me to Mesa Roja anymore." Maxie snuggled up to his big body, sated, warm and comfortable.

He put his arm around her, draping it casually across her flat stomach. "The chase is the interesting part, Maxie."

"Do you always have fun when you catch what you're chasing?" She ran her thumb along his collarbone, enjoying the heat of him against the sensitive pad of her fingertip.

Austin shifted, his voice hardened. "No. Usually I get paid."

And just like that they were back to square one. Releasing an uneven sigh, she met his gaze. "I can understand that you have a job to do. I really do."

"I can hear a but in there." His mouth was hard, his eyes bleak with the knowledge of how it would end for both of them.

"But I've caused my sister a lot of pain." Maxie raised herself up high enough so she could look him full in the face. There was wariness there and a look that said she wasn't going to change his mind. Undaunted, she continued to hold his gaze.

For a moment he stared into her eyes as if he were searching for something that was vital. Then he too let out a heavy sigh. ''Maxie, I want to save you, your sister and mine. But I...''

Resting her cheek against the top of his head, she swallowed hard and began slowly running her fingers through his hair. ''I understand that you don't want to go back on a promise you made to your sister. So you have to understand that I don't want to let Dorrie down. Dorrie is the only family I have that cares about me. You see it's been the two of us for a long time. My parents weren't much interested when we were little and left us mostly to our own devices. People liked to call Dorrie the serious bookworm and me the free spirit.''

She could feel his head nod. ''I do understand.''

''She's always been there when I needed her. Now it's my chance to be there for her. The opening of the nightclub is now a nightmare because of this embezzlement problem.

''She was the quintessential older sister. Dorrie used to walk me to school and pick me up. We spent a lot of time together since my mother was busy. She was a garden-party-set wannabe. She wanted Dorrie and I to fit in. I didn't. Dorrie did. While they were drinking tea, I'd sneak outside to play baseball with the next door neighbor's son. When they were all gathered around listening to Dorrie play the piano, I was climbing trees. I put frogs in my piano teacher's purse so she wouldn't come back. I was a hellion.''

''Why?''

''I guess to get attention so that my mother would see me for who I was, not what she wanted me to be. But she never did. When I was sixteen, I went to live with Dorrie because my mother told me constantly what a disappointment I was to her. When I graduated from college, I traveled around for a while and lived a bohemian lifestyle. I'd work until I got enough money to travel again. I never had a permanent address and I was constantly missing payments on my bills and Dorrie would cover me. I want all that to change now. I don't want her to have to pick up the pieces anymore.''

He rolled onto his back and dragged his hand down his face, then he turned his head and looked at her. And Maxie who had struggled to a sitting position with the sheet clutched around her, made an unnerving discovery. If she thought Austin was dangerous to her mental health when he was up and moving, he was really lethal all sleepy-eyed and sexy after a session of heavy lovemaking.

''Maxie,'' he whispered unevenly, rubbing at his eyes. ''I appreciate your dilemma. I really do.'' When he looked at her, she could see the indecision tearing him apart and it hurt her so much she actually had to steel her stomach.

''Now *I* hear a but.''

''Maxie. I won't be manipulated into giving up this bounty. I told you, I take my job seriously.''

Maxie closed her eyes and rested her forehead against her upraised knees, a stark feeling washed through her. Her answer was muffled. "Maybe you take everything *too* seriously."

When he didn't answer her, she raised her head. He was staring at her, and then he made a derisive sound and looked away, shaking his head in disgust.

"Maybe I do, but I don't know what else to do."

Maxie's stomach tightened at the look. "How about we table this discussion and try a bubble bath with those hot jets of water."

Austin breathed a sigh of relief. "That sounds good."

They got out of bed and went into the bathroom and Austin removed the cuffs. Maxie filled a quarter of the tub. Austin turned around to pick up some towels and that's when she saw the scar.

She reached out. "Is this where he stabbed you?"

He stiffened, but then relaxed. "Yes."

She leaned over and kissed the rough skin. "Were you ever in that much danger again?"

"Yes, but no one bested me like that again. I was too wary and started to build a reputation. Not many people wanted to mess with me."

"I don't blame them. Do you ever think about doing something else?"

"Yeah, I think about law enforcement."

"Think you might switch careers one day?"

"Maybe."

The warm water flowed over Austin's heated skin

as he lowered himself into the tub. Maxie climbed in and straddled him.

"Lean your head back." She picked up the portable shower nozzle and soaked his hair. Grabbing some shampoo, she washed his hair her fingers kneading his scalp. Austin breathed a sigh of pure contentment and she wondered how much he'd been pampered in his life. Not much, from what she could glean. She reached for his shaving kit and his eyes popped open.

"What? Don't trust me with a blade against your throat."

"I'd trust you with my life," he said softly and then closed his eyes again. With unbearable feelings swelling up in her chest, she applied shaving cream and then the razor gently to his skin. When she was finished, she used a washcloth and cleaned away the remnants of the shaving cream and whiskers.

She slipped off his lap and knelt between his legs, running her hands along his inner thighs.

"*Maxie,*" he groaned, "I don't think I can take any more. No more."

Austin's breath hissed in, and then he moaned deep in his chest as molten shards of pleasure ran quickly along his shaft when Maxie took him into her soft moist mouth.

Arching his hips uncontrollably in a primitive movement, he got lost in a dark haze as wave after wave of sensation drove him to the jagged edge.

He groaned, as she encircled the head of his swollen shaft with the tip of her tongue.

He thought he was going to explode.

Water, like a shimmering liquid rainbow, lapped gently around their heated bodies.

She rose, and with slow enticing movements, she climbed onto his lap, kneeling over his throbbing hardness. With slow, heated movements, she teased him with her succulent moistness, the tightly clustered curls an erotic goad each time she brushed sensually against him.

Unable to stand the compelling seductive assault, Austin shifted restlessly, his hands on her hips, his fingers moving rhythmically into her soft moist flesh. He dropped his head back, breathing hard. She moved wantonly against him again, and a low moan escaped him.

Maxie raised her hips and sank down onto his burning shaft, taking him deep inside her, crying out with gratification as she frantically glided over him.

His lips ached for her mouth, sought it in a mindless search. He kissed her with ravenous demand, sucking her into a turbulent maelstrom of spinning, whirling need, a dark realm of bliss. A tight knot of heat coiled low in his belly where her swollen flesh met his. With each driving thrust of his powerful hips, the heat escalated outward. Stardust tingled in his blood like glittering points of exhilarating heat.

She moved against him in wild abandon, driving him deeper and deeper, her motion faster and faster.

Austin captured a taut swollen nipple, sucking hard and urgently, moaning again when she arched her back in response to his hot mouth. Rapidly, with each rise and fall of her hips, his control escaped him. He let it go as he lost himself in the soft, yielding flesh, his tongue teasing each nipple into throbbing aching buds.

Her fingers dug into his shoulders and his elbow jerked from the wonderful feel of her response, hitting the control to the whirlpool.

Water surged out of power jet nozzles. Droplets cascaded down her pale, sleek body as she laughed delightedly, dropping her head back to feel the spray on her face. Captivated by her soft laughter, he watched her mouth, her eyes, rapt and beautiful, caught up in the savage pleasure he was giving her.

His mouth went back to her tantalizing breasts, and he licked at the shimmering rainbow droplets with his tongue, rubbing a provocative circle around the hard, beckoning tips.

And when his teeth nipped at each swollen bud, she writhed in ecstasy and he felt his own response to the fluttering spasms as he surged up to meet the descent of her hips.

He wanted to drive himself into her, make her his by sheer will as he rolled and brought her beneath him just as her climax subsided. Pushing her against the smooth white tub, Austin growled as he plunged into her, her body going soft and willing as she arched furiously to fill the empty space between them. Water sloshed against the sides of the tub from Austin's frantic movements.

She trembled beneath him and he asked huskily ''Are you cold?''

"No."

His body needed no further motivation as he responded with need, with possession. She was his, he'd made her his. The seduction of her hot naked body and the feel of warm liquid sliding like silk over his skin each time he thrust mindlessly into her, in turn, seduced him.

Her moans intensified with a breathless quality that pushed Austin closer and closer to his release. She tightened around him, and adjusted her legs to give him better access. The movement was almost more than he could bear, the pressure sweet agony.

She reached up and cupped his face, running her hands over the planes, the hot, slick skin of his face. Water streamed underneath her fingertips, dripping off his chin to drop onto her neck and face.

He felt as if the droplets were fragments of him, pieces that only she could mold, and that only her essence and skillful hands could keep together.

Her fingers slipped from his face and traced over the taut muscle of his biceps. His body tightened and released, and her name, drawn out in a long moan, burst from his throat. Sensation like an intense thrill of ecstasy jerked him in utter, mindless wonder as he spilled himself into her hot tightness.

Maxie clung to him, holding him so tightly around the neck that he could barely breathe as air gusted out of his lungs like a bellows. She felt like glittering sunshine exploding in a burst of bright white-hot light. Her head lay against his shoulder, her body still intimately joined to his.

He rose from the tub, bringing Maxie with him. Gently, he dried her and then dried himself off.

"It's getting late and we have a long way to go tomorrow. We'd better get some sleep."

She nodded and watched Austin settle down onto the mattress. Suddenly cold from the inside out, she wrapped her arms around herself, afraid that if she started to shiver she would never stop. She hated what she had to do to him, because she had feelings for him—bone-deep feelings that could only be one thing. She would not name it. It would be too much for her to overcome in the not too distant future. She would have to content herself with this time he'd so generously given them. It would be all they had because her plans didn't include being with Austin. He stood in her way and she had to do everything in her power to move him. If that meant using these new-found feelings he had for her, so be it. Only, it would kill her. It surely would kill her.

Maxie lay next to him and stared at the ceiling. As soon as she heard his heavy breathing, she located his cell phone. She pushed in the numbers and waited while the call connected. Even though she understood Austin, and compassion and tenderness for him existed in her heart, she knew that she still couldn't let her sister down.

There was no future between them. She'd been deluding herself into thinking that after her troubles were over, she and Austin could have some kind of a relationship. This could just be the beginning of her trouble.

Besides, Dorrie was her sister and she needed her right now. No one was going to stop her from protecting her sister, not even Austin.

It wasn't an easy decision to make. When Star answered, she could hear the sounds of the rowdy bar behind her. "The place is jumping tonight."

"Hi honey. Did you escape him again?"

Maxie felt much better when she heard Star's voice. Now here was someone who understood and took steps to help her. "No, not quite, but I will. I need to ask you a favor, but I want you to understand that this will be aiding and abetting a fugitive."

Star snorted. "Honey, tell me what you need. I'm a big girl, and I'm not afraid of any cops."

"I'm in Taos and I need your motorcycle. Can you do that?"

The click of glasses made it easy for Maxie to picture the rowdy bar. Sudden tears welled in her eyes. Damn, she missed the place.

She wiped the tears away as Star answered, "Sure honey. I can be there tomorrow night. What hotel?"

"Adobe and Pine Inn."

"Can you stall him that long?"

"Yes I can."

Maxie disconnected the call. She rolled onto her back and felt the tears well in her eyes again.

As if she could squeeze the feeling of despair that hung around her like a dark cloud, she wrapped her arms around herself. But other emotions clung to her and wouldn't let go—anger and shame, desperation and fear. Not even in this peaceful place could she throw off the tensions that surrounded her. The love-making with Austin had drained her, sapped her energy. She was in love with him. Cartwheeling, head-over-heels in love with him, and she couldn't tell him. In fact, she was leaving him, hurting him. She curled into herself for comfort.

She was now painfully aware that what she felt for Austin was something she'd never felt before. She hadn't intended to fall in love with him, and she didn't expect anything but heartache to follow. She was certain that making love with him had been a good idea and she was going to savor that taste and hoped it helped the heartache when she walked away from him.

This time she'd have to escape him for good.

WITH HIS CALLUSED PALMS holding her face, he kissed her awake with gentleness. Shifting her lower body into the embrace, her mind heavy with sleep, Maxie opened her mouth beneath the pressure, the sweetness of the caress. The warmth stimulated her, and she surrendered to the stirring kiss, lost in a thousand sensations. His mouth was so sweet and warm. So amazingly soft.

The hands released her, his mouth lifted from her and she felt the absence of its loss. A deep voice dissipated the last visages of sleep. "Rise and shine. It's time to go."

Feeling as if she were trying to clear cobwebs out of her brain, Maxie reluctantly opened her eyes, not wanting to let go of the sense of weightlessness.

When she opened her eyes, the first thing she noticed was that the cuffs were sitting on the nightstand and she thought fleetingly that he hadn't remembered to put them back on her. It seemed a telling mistake and she wondered suddenly if it had been a mistake at all. She moved closer still to his hot, muscular body and stretched.

He was wearing nothing but a towel and a sweet smile, his eyes smoldering with emotion. She took a deep breath and let it out.

"What time is it?"

"Six o'clock."

"Taggart, do you have a death wish?"

"That's a real scary threat, blondie." He laughed and smiled.

Still trying to come fully awake, she smiled back, loving the feel of his hands against her face. "Is that so? We're back to blondie?" she whispered sleepily.

The smile deepened. "I've decided that it suits you."

She narrowed her eyes and gave him a wicked smile. "I have some nicknames for you."

He grinned, then leaned over and gave her another one of those sweet, sweet kisses. "I bet you do, but they can't be repeated in public."

His smile and bright, twinkling eyes were irresistible. "I bet you think you're something, Taggart."

"Yeah, I do."

He cupped her face, bringing his mouth close to her lips, his touch making her tremble. "You look so comfortable. It's a shame."

She reached up and touched his warm cheek. "What's a shame?"

Before she realized what he had in mind, he rolled off the bed taking the blanket and sheet with him. Maxie grabbed for it, catching the corner. Austin's strength was too much for her and he dragged the blanket, sheet and her to the floor. He leaned his shoulder to the wall and held up the blanket, a tormenting grin on his face. "That."

"You are such a jerk," she said, huffing with laughter. "Give me back that blanket."

He held it up to display. "This blanket."

"Austin," she warned, lunging for the blanket. He snatched it from her reach. His grin broadened, and he tossed the blanket across the room, and then blocked her way so she couldn't get to it. "Nope. It's time to go." He glanced toward the bathroom and then at her.

"Seems to me you need a wake up call."

"No, Austin." She started to giggle. "No cold showers for me."

"Yes, Francesca. I think it's what you need."

The thought occurred to her that if she taunted him and then was able to win, she could delay him one more day. It hurt her, but she had to make the decision and she had to make it now. "Want to bet. You have to give me another day here and no battles when I win."

He laughed. "No battles."

Maxie went on the offensive. She reached up and snatched the towel from around his waist and flung the wet terry around his feet and yanked. Austin went down, while she made a beeline for the bathroom door and the wonderful, safe lock on the other side. He caught her ankle and brought her beneath him as he covered her naked body in one swift, powerful move. "I win. Time's awasting. Time for a shower."

"I'm not under the cold spray, yet," she challenged. She fought against his hold convulsing with laughter. She got her fingers under his ribs and found out that Austin was quite ticklish. He grabbed for her hand twisting his body and that gave her enough space to use her leg as leverage and flip him off her. She rose quickly, and was off to the bathroom again. Austin recovered fast, his reflexes honed and sharp. At the door, he grabbed her shoulder, spun her and hoisted her over his shoulder with an ease that astounded her. His voice breaking with laughter and exertion, he tried to haul her into the bathroom. "You are a resourceful little thing."

In desperation, she grabbed for the door frame on either side of his heavily muscled body. She struggled with all her might, her laughter weakening her. "No Austin. I hate to be cold." She was losing her grip on the door frame, and he only had to take a few steps to the gleaming shower and he'd have her in there.

Securing her legs with one big arm, he grabbed one wrist and tried to break her hold on the door frame. "Tough. A bet is a bet."

She knew it was only a matter of time. Giggling and out of breath, she braced her chest against his back and brought her hand hard against the firm flesh of his backside. "Ouch! You little viper!"

With just one arm on her legs, it was easy for her to kick free and slide down his back. Knowing she had to disable him or he would consider the contest still in progress, she seized him around the calves and used her shoulder against the backs of his knees. He let out a yell and went down like Goliath after David's attack. Still laughing, she smacked him on the behind again and said, "You really do have a nice butt."

He rolled over onto his back, his chest rising and falling with laughter also. "Dammit, blondie, I didn't know you were a street fighter."

She grinned at him. "Well, now you do."

Smiling an irresistible smile, he reached down and slipped his hands under her arms and dragged her up the length of his body. She braced her elbows on his chest and rested her chin on her hands. His presence was all around her. The smell of his skin. The feel of the hot flesh of his chest against her breasts, his shaft against her pubic bone, the smoothness of his legs as she straddled him. She gazed down into his eyes, the sweet, enticing color of honey. There was a depth to him that she could see in his eyes, a fullness that was ripe, poignant and which made her heart contract with pain.

Lost in his eyes, she knew in that heartbreaking moment that she'd run out of time. There was no more for him and her. In a matter of twenty-four-hours, she would be gone and her actions would drive this man away from her. In the wake of her betrayal, all his feelings would dry up and die for her.

Closing her eyes against the sudden burst of pain, she slid her arms around his neck and held on to him, the sense of loss so consuming, knowing she could be saying goodbye to him for the very last time.

But she had to. It didn't matter that she wanted every single minute from now on to be spent with him. Once she did this, he would be too hurt and betrayed to want anything from her at all. That thought filled her chest to overflowing, made her eyes sting, and her heart break. She thought it might break forever.

As if sensing the change in her, Austin framed her face with his palms, his voice full of regret. He murmured, "I don't have any choice, Maxie. I have to bring you in."

Her jaw tightened against the cramp in her throat, she slipped her arms around him, willing away the stinging fullness burning her eyes. She didn't dare think about what she had to do and how he would never forgive her. She would never get through the next short while if she did. Inhaling deeply, she buried her face into the hollow of his throat, trying to gather her strength and purpose around her. Enough to get her through this. Enough to hold her together.

Austin let out a ragged, uneven breath and eased his hand up her back, then turned his head and kissed her temple. "Don't, Maxie," he whispered roughly.

Giving into his request, she swallowed hard and

pinched him lightly on the arm. "You lost, Taggart. That means you have to give me the whole day."

He chuckled and rubbed his hand across her hips, pressing her firmly against his groin. "My first mistake was making the bet at all. I should have realized what I was up against."

Reaching down for a smile, she raised her head and looked at him, gazing into his eyes. "What was your second mistake?"

He grinned and slid his hand across her buttocks. "Pulling you on top of me."

She gave him a dry, steady look. "Too bad because I think there's another issue coming up between us."

His gaze was warm and intimate; he stared at her, his eyes alive with delight. Then something hot and dangerous flickered in his gaze.

AUSTIN WAS TRULY at odds on how to resist this golden goddess straddling his hips, making his erection throb with the desire to sheathe himself in her to the hilt. She was simply everything he could ever want, and to a man who rarely took, it was torture.

They were at quite a huge impasse. She didn't want to go back to Sedona and he had to take her back. She would never forgive him and he was sure she would never want to have anything more to do with him.

He was really beginning to chafe against the sense of honor that was keeping him from everything he wanted. His sense of duty warred with his need to protect Maxie from the law, from herself. He wanted to wrap her in a cocoon and stand guard so that no one could ever hurt her again. But he was going to be the one who hurt her the most. That thought tore at his heart and made him ready to agree to anything she asked of him, short of promising not to take her back. He could give her one more day. What would it hurt in the big scheme of things?

He pressed his thumb against her mouth, trying his damnedest to maintain the trace of a smile. "There's nothing I want more than to deal with that issue, but what about the other issue?"

Cupping his hand against the angle of her jaw, he stroked her ear and brushed a soft kiss against her forehead. Smoothing down some spiky wisps of hair, Austin rested his head against hers, a solemn, thoughtful expression appearing. He stared off into the distance, then inhaled and spoke, gently caressing her ear. "The issue that I'm still taking you back."

"Austin, why do we have to worry about that now? Why can't we just live in the moment. Be together and have fun. Don't spoil it."

"I always do my job, Maxie, and it used to be easy." His throat suddenly closed up on him, and he tightened his hold on her face, hugging her head against the curve of his shoulder. He had to wait for the tightness to ease, and then he spoke, his voice husky with emotion. "I didn't bargain on you."

"Why are you so responsible?" she asked, her voice subdued.

There was a brief silence, his voice oddly quiet. "I

try to be what I think my father would want me to be.''

Maxie's grip around his neck tightened, shock coursed through her. She had been sure Austin's motives had nothing to do with monetary gain and everything to do with the support of his family, but she had no idea that his sense of responsibility was tied up with his need to be what his father expected of him. ''Oh Austin, why do you have to be so unpredictable?''

''I am?''

Maxie closed her eyes, praying that she could keep her voice from breaking. ''Yes, you are. You're a much better person than I am.''

''No, I'm not. You're doing all this to save *your* sister.''

''Jessica has this great opportunity to study in Paris,'' Maxie said, her voice full of pain. ''It could mean the beginning of a very lucrative career for her doing something she loves. But that's not why you're doing this. You promised her that she could go. You'd never back down from that promise and neither would your dad. Would he?''

He shook his head. It all became extremely clear to her. Austin did understand her need to help and protect her sister because he was doing the exact same thing. She couldn't think badly of him for it. ''You've done so much for your family, haven't you?'' Maxie whispered unevenly.

''I didn't think about it. I just thought about what

my father would do and whether it was hard or not, I did it. I wanted him to be proud of me.''

''I'm sure he is. Austin, what was the real reason you left to live with your grandmother?'' She should stop asking because she felt this wad of emotion building in the back of her throat. This information would only make what she had to do harder.

''My stepfather wasn't a tolerant man, especially with someone else's kid. I think he was jealous of the attention my mother gave me, and he made her feel as if it was making me a weak boy and, therefore, a weak man. She withdrew quite a bit. It hurt so much. I resented him and deep down I resented her for loving someone who wasn't my father. This man could never take his place. When we came to blows, I saw how that affected my mother. So I left to live with my grandmother.''

Maxie closed her eyes, trying to get her brain around the sheer selfless acts of the man she clasped to her.

She reached out and touched his face, a swell of emotion rising in her. ''You humble me, Austin. You truly do.''

There was a brief pause, and then Austin spoke again. ''I was devastated when my father died. I don't think I've ever gotten over it.''

She tried to clear a cramp in her throat and that wad of emotion expanded. ''When you loved your father as much as you do, you never do.''

''I've never told anyone what I just told you. You are a formidable woman.''

Her head came up and she stared at him, trying to infuse some humor back into the conversation. "Little ol' me?"

A warped smile appearing, he ran his hands over the tantalizing spikes of her blonde hair. "Yeah," he said, his voice husky. "You." She kept looking at him, and Austin ran his thumb down her cheek, a tight feeling unfolding in his chest.

"It's time we were on the road back to Sedona."

She reached out and captured his forearm. At her touch, he stilled, the muscles bunching beneath her palm. She smiled and said, "What's your hurry? You lost a bet, pal, and I intend to collect."

"Maxie…" was all the protest he got out as she cut him off.

"I'd much rather deal with this *hard* issue right now." Sliding her hand down his body, she took a hold of his erection and squeezed. "Then we're going to have some fun today. Right?"

He looked up. Something painful happened around his heart when he realized that turning her in would tear him apart. That after he did so, his life would be very bleak and empty. He wished there was a way he could keep his honor intact and get her off the hook. He wished for a way out of this horrible mess. He wanted Maxie in his life, but with the act of turning her in, he would seal his fate and hers. She would hate him and he'd be alone and loving her for the rest of his life.

It was the kind of love that his father had had for

his mother. He recognized it in him and knew there was no way it would fade. Not this time.

Moving his hand along her jaw until his fingers were buried in her hair, he drew her head down, the fullness in his chest making his throat cramp. With minimal pressure, he brushed his mouth over hers in slow sweeps. "I want to be inside you," he whispered unevenly against her mouth. "Deep, deep inside."

Releasing her pent-up breath in a rush, Maxie pushed away from him.

She rose up, and the pressure on his erection made him turn his head, releasing something raw and uncontrollable inside him.

She peered into the bedroom and snagged the condom box from the floor where it had been dropped.

Gasping raggedly, he clasped her against him. A tremor coursed through her, and she drew her knees up and pulled out of his hold. She sat back, sliding her hips from side to side, then lifted up enough to roll a condom down his erection.

Becoming aware of what she was going to do, he snatched her hand away. "Not on the floor, Maxie."

She rotated enough to free her wrist, forcing his hands down by his head. She shuddered as she rose up, and then lowered herself upon him, taking him deep inside her. Deep, deep inside her.

Feeling as if he was going to come out of his skin, Austin hardened his jaw against the breathtaking rush of feeling. His shoulders lifted off the floor as she moved her hips in a slow, sliding dance, causing his heart to beat hard in his chest. With his pulse thick and heavy, her hands now moving to intertwine with his fingers, he turned his head against the hardness of the floor.

"Maxie, not on the floor. The bed…wait."

With a deliberate movement she lowered her breasts in a silken, erotic glide across his chest. "No," she whispered brokenly. "I can't wait." Another tremor shook her body and the movement of her hips increased in tempo. She tightened her hold on his hands. Curving her hips against him, her breath caught as she rose then sheathed him with her hot, wet tightness.

Sucking in a breath through clenched teeth, an agony of sensation coursed through him. He wanted to get up and move them to the more comfortable bed. Maxie deserved better than this raw sex on the floor.

Maxie took him deeper inside her and all his thoughts shattered like glass, the hard wave of sheer bliss took him. He groaned and twisted beneath her, loosening his hands he grabbed her hips.

Maxie sobbed into his mouth, "You on top," her hands clutching at him, and she lifted her hips, rolling her pelvis hard against him.

"Maxie. The bed."

"No. Please, Austin."

Giving in, he rolled. She cried out when he pulled out of her and all but dragged her from the bathroom onto the cushioned carpet of the bedroom.

She writhed beneath him, her arms coming up to hold him in place, but like smoke, he wafted down her body, his hands sliding along her inner thighs. He opened her wide and clamped his mouth against the wet, hot bud of her sex.

She cried out and bucked against his mouth. Finding her sensitized nub, he pleasured her with his mouth until she was moaning and writhing, moving wildly against him. Her movements grew frantic, her muscles coiled tight and rigid. Reflexively she pressed her legs against his face. She moaned and her inner muscles clenched. He took her all in a deep, wild kiss, at the same time probing more deeply with his tongue. She whimpered at the dual assault.

His control shredded when he felt her delicate convulsions against his tongue. He surged up her body and thrust into her before she finished climaxing.

She made another wild sound, and her counter-thrusts turned reckless and uneven. Austin pulled her to him, his body on fire, his senses overloading. Moving now on pure instinct and need, he kept thrusting into her, fighting the rising, expanding tide inside him.

Maxie wrapped her legs around his hips, drawing him deeper inside her. His body throbbed with a hunger of its own as she exploded with a soft, low cry. Unable to hold out with the feel of her pulsing around him, he released a ragged groan, going stiff and letting go, emptying himself deep inside her. Clutching her to him, he held her head against him, her face wet against his neck. Shredded inside, he pressed his mouth against her forehead and closed his eyes, his pulse irregular and jerky, and the feelings in his chest unbearable. He didn't know what he was going to do without her.

With a slow and comforting touch he softly stroked the soft, damp tangle of her hair. Drawing in a deep breath, he cupped her face with his hands. Realizing that she needed something to lessen the intense emotion, he tilted her head back and trailed a light kiss across her lips, letting a touch of humor surface.

"Okay, you convinced me. How do you want to spend the day?"

9

AUSTIN EYED the white beast with the black coloring around his eyes.

"Go ahead, pet him, he doesn't bite." The guide urged.

The soft humming of the animal was very soothing and Austin reached out to touch the animal's neck. He twitched his ears and the humming increased. The wool was soft and springy.

"Maxie, when you asked me if I wanted to take a llama to lunch, I thought you were out of your mind."

"Bandit is going to carry our gourmet lunch while we hike along and enjoy the Sangre de Cristo Mountains."

The guide began speaking telling the day hikers to watch out for wildlife especially black bears, elk, mountain lions and rattlesnakes. The guide indicated that the llamas would alert the hikers to any dangers with their high-pitched cry.

They started out walking side by side up the slope, the trail worn by many feet, both two-legged and four-legged. To either side of the path a carpet of wildflowers bloomed. Austin stopped and squatted. He fingered a delicate yellow flower. He looked up at Maxie, who'd stopped when he did. "These are buttercups, also called columbine—any flower in the buttercup family. The Apache used the seeds of this flower to cure headaches and fever."

Intrigued, Maxie walked over to a small daisylike flower. "What's this?"

"Groundsel." Austin rose and walked over to stand next to Maxie. The curious look on her face reminded him of a young child, free and inquisitive, reveling in the wonder of nature. "Apaches used this to treat open wounds."

"And this?" Maxie toed a clump of small blue to purplish flower with the toe of her new hiking boot.

"Pennyroyal. It's more than a pretty little flower. The oil found in the flower is an excellent insect repellent and a tea made from the plant was once thought to be a cure for a variety of illnesses."

"Your grandmother taught you this stuff, didn't she?"

"As I told you," he said, looking off into the background of a variety of spruce, fir and aspen trees rising up against the blue mammoth of Wheeler's Peak. It was breathtaking scenery, where the mountains met the sky, a bigger, bluer and more fascinating living canvas than any other place Austin had been. He admired the scenery for a few more moments then turned his face back to Maxie. "She was a medicine woman for my tribe."

"The connection you have to your family and your ancestors must make you feel grounded."

"I never thought of it in those terms, but it does make me feel secure."

"The only person in my life who made me feel grounded was Dorrie."

"That's sad that your parents didn't know who you were. They missed out."

Maxie slid her arm through his, and it made him feel grounded, too. She smiled up at him. "What else. Tell me more of your mystical grandmother's wisdom."

"I will if you tell me more about your family."

"There really isn't much to tell. My father is a really boring upper-middle-class accountant and, as I told you, my mother a social butterfly that is more important than anything in her life, even her daughters. Even if we had some interesting family ancestors, my mother wouldn't care about sharing that with me. Once she realized that I wasn't going to be what she wanted me to be, she gave up on me and focused on Dorrie. She did use it against me, though."

He nodded as they caught up to the group, who were admiring a spectacular view of Taos and the valley beyond. "I'm sorry. I know how you feel. My stepfather wasn't too keen on me either."

Soon they continued their journey through the mountains, the guide pointing out places of interest.

No matter how he tried, he couldn't get Bandit to leave his side. She kept leaning over and rubbing her nose against his face, which was the equivalent of a llama kiss the amused guide informed him.

It was almost noon, the third time the animal did it, and he heard Maxie laugh softly.

"You think it's funny?" he asked, amusement tugging at the corners of his mouth when he gave Bandit a quick pat on the neck. The animal began to hum louder in contentment.

"I think she likes you, Austin," Maxie said, moving closer to him and companionably sliding her arm around his waist. Her eyes were alight with a twinkling amusement, her face animated.

But when hadn't she been bubbly and happy. Even when she was fighting with him, she had that same animation. The woman loved life, lived it to the fullest extent. Whereas he...well, he didn't. He might be a bounty hunter facing danger in his job, but had he really lived or just existed? From the moment he'd met her she'd made him feel alive.

His chest filled and he put his arm around her shoulder and drew her close, thinking that a woman like Maxie would stop the years stretching out in front of him from seeming bleak.

The sudden intrusion of Bandit's nose between him and Maxie, then her head, which effectively pushed Maxie away and separated them, made not only laughter bubble from her, but from the other hikers, as well.

"It seems that Bandit's jealous," the guide said.

Austin laughed with good nature. What did he care if the beast showed her affection? It had made Maxie laugh and he was sure that he cared about that. The sound of it made his chest tighten. It was his own fault if he felt as protective of Maxie as the llama felt protective of him. For the first time, he allowed the idea of letting her go become a full-fledged thought in his head. Yet, the consequences of his action would compromise not only his principles, but also Jessica's plans. Not that he could compare Jessica's trip to France to the trouble that Maxie faced in Sedona. They were not the same things at all.

But could he let her go? Could he really loosen some of his ironclad principles? It was his father who had instilled such traits in him and it was a way he could keep him alive. A heaviness settled on Austin's heart when he thought about his father. Would he be proud of a son who threw his resolve into the wind and relinquished his responsibilities to his family and his job?

It was something he contemplated the rest of the day as they made their way back to Taos and a night out on the town.

As THEY ENTERED the pueblo-style adobe restaurant the walls made from sun-dried clay bricks mixed with grass for strength, mud-mortared and covered with additional protective layers of mud, Maxie slipped her arm through Austin's. He smiled down at her as if they were a couple enjoying the nightlife.

The hostess led them past an adobe-brick kiva fireplace to a table, but Maxie protested. "Do you think we could eat outside?" The hostess smiled and turned away from the booth. They went through an arched doorway stenciled with red and green chiles that opened onto a patio. The support beams of the restaurant extended out to form a makeshift roof without the thatching. Twinkling white lights intertwined with the rough and ready beams called vigas, which lent a romantic air to the already enchanted night.

The hostess placed the menus on the table and said, "Your server will be with you in a moment." Then the woman walked through the door that led into the restaurant.

Maxie picked up and opened the menu full of Hispanic and Pueblo cuisine. There was the regular fare of enchiladas, burritos and tacos served with bean or *frijoles refritos,* beans mashed and refried in oil. But there were also other dishes not usually found in traditional Hispanic food, like empanada, a fried pie with nuts and currants and posole, a corn soup or stew prepared with pork and chile. For dessert she wanted a sopaipillas, a lightly fried puff pastry served with honey.

Moving her eyes from the menu, she gazed up to the heavens. "This is perfect," Maxie breathed.

Austin followed her gaze up to the night sky, carpeted with brilliant stars. There was a sad look on his face.

"Why do you look so sad?"

He picked up the menu and opened it, shrugging his shoulders as if trying to ward off a chill. But Maxie could sense that her question struck at something that went much deeper than a chill on the skin.

She looked up at the stars. "What is it, Austin?"

"Just something I remembered about my dad."

Austin looked at her with an odd kind of hesitancy. It seemed as if he would speak and then the moment passed and he closed down.

"What?" she prompted, knowing now that she must hear what he had to say. "Tell me."

He closed his eyes, clenching his hands into fists on the table. He drew in a long, shuddery breath. "We used to go out on nights like this, drive to a remote area where there was very little light, and lie on the hood of his car."

"To look at the stars?"

"Yeah." He broke off as if he was searching for the words or they were too painful to remember. He cleared his voice. "They fascinated me. One of those nights I mentioned to him that it would be cool to look through a telescope so I could see them better."

He drew a long, rough breath. "That Christmas, guess what was under the tree."

"A telescope."

"A telescope. I couldn't wait for night to fall. It was cold, but he took me back to our lookout place and we set up the telescope. It was…amazing, seeing the stars through the lens, and it made it more… special because he was there."

Maxie reached out and squeezed his forearm. "How old were you?"

"Ten. It was the year he died."

For a moment, the silence stretched between them. Her chest felt full to bursting. "Do you still have the telescope?"

"No. I still remember what he said to me, though."

"What?"

Austin stared at Maxie for a moment, then looked down at his menu, his expression fixed and sober. "The sky's the limit and I should reach for the stars," he answered, his tone subdued.

"Like the FBI?"

Austin turned his gaze from the menu he was reading and looked at her. Shutters snapped shut over yearnings and remorse. "Water under the bridge. I don't brood over what was lost, Maxie. I do what needs to be done regardless of the consequences."

"Or the sacrifices you have to make?" Her voice was rough with emotion, her tone soft with kindness.

Austin's jaw clenched. "That's right."

"Am I a sacrifice?"

He swallowed and looked away from her, then back up to the stars as if they could save him.

"Yes," he softly answered but like a shout it broke Maxie's heart.

"I thought so. It's flattering."

He laughed but it held no mirth. "That's something she would have said."

"Who?"

"Shelly. The other skip that got into my jeans so that I would let her go."

"Did you?"

Austin gave her a long, level look and a menacing smile. "No. I tracked her down and brought her back. At the time, I thought she really cared for me, but she didn't. She was tricking me the whole time."

Guilt grabbed her, clawing at her gut for the way

she planned to trick Austin. The server interrupted her thoughts and Maxie ordered a margarita, telling the server that she wanted a bowl of posole with *pan dulce,* a Native American sweet bread along with the sopaipillas. Austin ordered Carne adovada, tender pork marinated in red chili sauce, herbs and spices and then baked. He also ordered a margarita.

She had to escape Austin, and tricking him was the only way she could do it, because he wasn't going to voluntarily let her go. The thought of letting Dorrie down brought tears to her eyes. The choice wasn't one anyone should have to make. Betray this man who had come to mean everything to her or the sister of her blood and her heart, a sister who had taken the brunt of all Maxie's shenanigans and pulled her out of the fire time and time again. This was her chance to save her sister. She had to make that choice and give up what she now realized would be an incredible life with a man she understood in every way. But she could not fail her sister, not this time. Not again. "I'm sorry that she hurt you, Austin."

She saw something flicker in his eyes, a darkness skimming that honey brown like the shadow of a passing crow. "I believe that you are," he said softly, looking away.

She flashed him a scowl. "Are you trying to change the subject?"

"What subject would that be?"

Maxie was interrupted when the waitress brought them two huge, frothing glasses of margaritas. She took a sip to gather her strength and to cool her parched throat. The salt burst on her tongue mixing with the hot, tantalizing taste of tequila and tang of lime.

Austin followed suit and Maxie was fascinated at the way his throat moved, the muscles contracting as he swallowed. Even though she'd shaved him this morning, the dark stubble was back and only enhanced his dangerous, renegade look.

"You're not off the hook, Taggart."

For a minute there she thought he was going to address her question, but his eyes darkened. "What hook would that be?"

"The one where you tell me all about how you sacrificed your dreams for your family."

Austin sighed. "So, I gave up the FBI for my fifteen-year-old sister and my mother. So what?"

"So what? They were more important than your dreams. That's what. Not many men would have done that."

Austin looked at her silently.

"What happened?"

"I told you I joined the army right out of high school."

"You said you were an MP. Did you see any combat? You're too young to have been in the Gulf War."

"I did a few stints overseas, but I didn't see any combat."

"How did you get out of the service?"

"I asked for a hardship discharge and it was granted." He took another sip of his drink.

"Then what happened?" she asked, wondering at the light stain on his cheeks. He was embarrassed about what he had done for his family.

"I told you what happened. I became a bounty hunter."

"What happened with the FBI?"

"What do you mean?"

Maxie stiffened at his don't-go-there tone.

"How close were you to joining?" she persisted as she watched his eyes darken even more.

"You are like a hurricane. Can't fly around it, can't avoid it. You have to meet it dead on." He looked up at the sky again, his eyes lingering as if caressing a lover. "The call from the training department came on the heels of the call from my grandmother."

Maxie felt his answer at the center of her chest, a gentle throb that flickered and flared like a candle. He'd been so close. She ached at the pain in his eyes, the hard contest in his expression. She heard the faint echo of need in his voice and felt herself slipping even more between that rock and hard place. "That must have been so painful."

He closed his eyes and said, "Leave it alone, Maxie. It's over. I made my choice and I haven't regretted it."

"You sacrificed everything for your family," she whispered on a ragged sigh. How could she do any less for her sister? But damn the man. Damn him for walking into her life. She thought about what he had done. It humbled her. It was enough to make a person cry. It was enough to make a woman fall in love.

And she would just have to be that woman.

Damn him.

AFTER THE DELICIOUS dinner was over, Austin and Maxie walked down the dusty streets coming once again to the edge of the Kit Carson Park. She grinned at him, a full, tantalizing, sucker-punch-to-the-gut kind of smile. The same kind Austin was sure Delilah used right before she showed Samson the shears.

"Look familiar?"

"It's the place where we lost ourselves in the rain last night." The memory of her soft flesh against his fingertips did crazy things to his insides.

"It's a good thing the cops couldn't see us through all this foliage." Wheeler Peak was a dusky outline in the dark northern sky.

She turned to him and picked up his hand, kissing the backs of his fingers.

"Where do we go from here?

He cupped her face. "I wish I knew."

"You really don't see any way around it, Austin."

"I really wish I could, but it's more than just taking you in. I think you know that now." He paused, and staring into her face, he could see that she understood and it made his insides clench because no one, not even his mother had ever understood why he would give up so much.

"It's all tied up in your need to make your father proud."

It was. He'd already acknowledged that to himself.

She folded her arms and with quick, brisk movement rubbed at the goose bumps pebbling her skin.

"Cold?" He took off his shirt, leaving him only in a black T-shirt. He arranged the material around her shoulders, coaxing her arms into the sleeves.

"It's so warm. Warm from your skin and it smells like you, so good. But won't you be cold?"

Her voice was soft and subdued mingling with the sigh of the wind and the hard beat of his heart.

He was so preoccupied with his own pain-filled memories that he had to take a deep breath before he could speak. "No."

Starting at the bottom, he gathered the shirttails together and began to button it. The back of his hands brushed against her stomach in a game of silent torture that made his body tighten. When he reached her breastbone, she made a soft gasp as he accidentally caught the tip of her breast with his forefinger.

He knew that sound, had heard her express her excitement, her desire for him. His fingers twisted in the cotton as more than desire settled in the pit of his stomach, so much more it made his heart burn.

"I had such a beautiful day with you, Austin."

Austin concentrated on getting the last few buttons done. He raised his head and looked into her eyes. They were so blue and deep. "I did, too." She cupped his face, her hand sliding along his skin. Austin thought, this is it. What he wanted. This woman.

Her hair shone in the moonlight, like a shiny star fallen to earth. Austin's hands went to the silky mass and slid through the strands of hair.

Enslaved by the silkiness of her hair and the caressing feel of her hot palm against his cheek, he knew he had to share with her what he had never told another living soul.

"Do you know," he said, "my ancestors believed that it was taboo to say a dead person's name. That by doing so you conjure up a ghost." Knowing his words would release a dreaded and horrible pain he'd harbored for years, he felt safe in her presence. "Maybe all this time he's been haunting me and I should put him to rest. Let go of my anger and resentment because he died."

She shifted closer to him, pressing her face against his chest, wrapping her arms around his neck as if she sensed this was hurting him.

"That's not easy."

Her voice was indistinct as if she spoke through water. "No, it's not." He took a deep breath and asked, "Remember, at dinner I told you I didn't have the telescope anymore."

"Yes."

"I was so angry at him. I smashed it until it was unusable. Afterwards, I was ashamed and felt even worse."

"Oh God, Austin." She pulled away from him to look up into his face, but he looked straight ahead, the memories dark and chaotic. She tightened her hold on him, her skin so warm against him. So comforting, an oasis in a vast, empty wasteland.

"I'm so sorry," she whispered, her voice ragged and raw against him. "I feel…" She tried to shake her head as if it could break the words free. It only tormented Austin with the silken soft whisper of her hair against his skin. ''But this isn't real. Any of it. We're the only two people in the world, right now. I can't want you without paying the consequences.''

Austin straightened, reached down to lift her face to him, gathering his composure. Surprised that he had told her about the telescope, he'd somehow healed. ''The consequences?''

He would have rather died than cause the pain he found in those eyes. He hated himself, knowing that he couldn't take it away. Knowing now, that he couldn't shirk his responsibilities to his family or to his job. He'd take her in no matter what. He wanted more time with her, but it seemed that their time had run out.

''The consequences would be one of us has to lose and it's not fair, but that's the truth. One of us has to lose.''

''I know.''

''This day is just an interlude…a break in the battle.''

''That's not a bad thing.''

She smiled and held his face, her hands soft as she traced his cheekbone with her thumb. ''Now you're getting it, Taggart.'' A twinkle appeared in her eyes. She broke away from him and led him towards his car.

''Where are we going?'' He put on the breaks and stopped her in the middle of the street.

''Now it's time to lose that responsible nature of

yours, Austin, and do something reckless.'' She tugged on him again and drew him forward.

"I think I've been reckless enough for one day."

"The day's not over."

Austin laughed. He couldn't help it. She was irresistible. "Just a moment. Before I run recklessly toward whatever you have in store for me..." He stopped and kissed her sweet, enticing mouth. "Now will you tell me where we're going?"

"You'll see. Just stop when I say so."

It was minutes later when she asked him to pull over and he did. With a smile, she got out of the car and Austin followed her. Then he saw the storefront and groaned. "Maxie, a tattoo?"

"Sure."

She left the sidewalk and pushed the door open. Austin shut the door to his car and followed her. Inside, the lights were very bright. Colorful pictures of possible tattoos were all over the wall. Maxie was already talking to the woman behind the counter who had many a body part pierced.

She turned and gave him a wink. "So which one would you like?"

Austin looked at the tattoos as the woman took his arm and sat him in a chair. "How about an eagle?"

"An eagle? That's boring," Maxie said, her eyes lit up. Before he could stop her, she was out the door. He tried to get past the woman in front of him, but she blocked his way. It was only seconds later that Maxie came back into the shop. In her hands was his grandmother's hand-wrought shield.

"Can you do this?" Maxie asked.

The woman studied the shield and smiled. "Sure can."

Something tight and hot settled in Austin's chest. He barely felt the first prick of the tattoo tool as it injected ink into the skin of his upper arm. He was looking at Maxie and the shield wishing that he could protect both his family and her.

But he knew that the choice had already been made.

His grandmother's words came back to him in a rush. *"I dreamed that you were chasing the sun."*

His response came back to him. *"Is there danger in this, Grandmother?"*

"Yes, of a kind, but one you will battle and overcome because you have the soul of a great warrior." The soul of a great warrior? He didn't know about that, but he knew what he had to do. Knowing it didn't make it any easier.

Maxie chose a red-gold blazing sun and asked the pierced woman to tattoo the symbol around her naval.

It was then that he remembered his grandmother's caution.

"You cannot catch the sun without getting burned."

10

HE LAY NEXT TO MAXIE and tried to pretend. He tried really, really hard to pretend that she didn't mean a thing to him, that if he were only minutes from Sedona, he'd take her right to the jail and drop her off, collect his bounty and go home. He'd go home and get a cold beer and thank his lucky stars that she—that this bounty—was behind him.

The soft chime of his cell phone made him reach out and flip open the phone. He glanced over at Maxie, but she was still asleep.

"Hello?" His voice came out hoarse from disuse.

"Austin."

"Mom." He sat up higher in bed. "What's wrong?" His mother never called him on the job unless it was serious.

"Austin, I haven't heard from you in a few days. Are you all right? Is everything okay?"

"Don't worry, Mom. I'm fine. I'm taking care of everything."

His mother's voice was subdued when she responded. "Take care. You're always on my mind."

He turned away so that Maxie wouldn't hear. "I love you all. I'll be home soon."

He didn't remember when he'd started thinking of her as Maxie and less as "blondie." But he had.

He put the phone on the nightstand and sank back down. Closing his eyes intensified her exotic scent. That sweet scent he would never get enough of and never forget. It seemed to have seeped into him permanently.

It was quiet outside, except for the soft chirping of the birds. Quiet outside, but inside he was in turmoil. She'd been trouble and she had snagged a part of him he'd never known he had to give.

Besides the needs that clamored inside him, one ugly fact still remained: He didn't want to let her go.

He was thankful that in his weakness he hadn't made emotional admissions and confessions he couldn't take back. He needed her in ways less basic, more intricate than the mere physical, but caving in to those needs, his primitive desires, seemed like jumping from the frying pan into the fire.

It was easy to daydream. He used to do it a lot. Daydream that his father hadn't died and they were all still a family. Daydream that he had been able to fulfill his dream and make a difference as an FBI agent. But he couldn't daydream himself out of this dilemma. He had to bring her in even though he wanted to become part of her, integral to her life for the rest of time, the way he had the uncomfortable, despairing feeling that she'd become critical to his well-being, his sanity—only he was going to wind up losing her. If he brought her in, he'd lose her. If he let her go, he'd lose her. He may have lost his purpose in thinking he could give up the bounty and let her go, but the call from his mother reminded him that he did have responsibilities to provide for and care for his family.

He'd lose again and in that moment between one breath and the next, he knew why he'd never taken, never wanted and let his dreams flow through his hands like water. He'd been afraid of losing, the way he'd lost his father, and then his mother to his stepfather. He'd kept his distance from his family, never fully embraced them and their love. Not even Jessica, because he was afraid all three of them would exit his life just like his father, leaving him alone.

There was a deep, empty well inside him, one he could fill with Maxie so easily. He wanted her to fill him. He opened his eyes and turned his head.

His heart contracted and he sighed heavily. She was exquisite, lying in wild, naked abandon—her smooth arms over her head, her sweet lips slightly parted, her golden blond hair spiked and sexy.

He reached over and under the bed, where he'd secreted the key. Very gently, he unlocked the cuffs and set both the key and cuffs on the nightstand.

Then he moved over her, and as if her mouth were a beacon in a dark, cold, lonely night, he took it. Her lips were a hot, wet invitation, a hint of secrets and pleasures to be revealed. He took it roughly, parting her lips with his tongue and moving inside, claiming her. She met his foray with enthusiasm and longing. She took his face between her hands to draw him closer, deeper, sent her tongue into his mouth on a sensual mission.

He groaned, a daring sound full of hunger, a call to her heart. She moaned, an edgy sound filled with yearning, a reply that left no doubt to her feelings.

Kneeling on the bed between her legs, he caught the underside of her knees and drew her towards him. She encircled his hips and locked her ankles, looped her elbows around his neck and pulled his chest flat against the sweet, yielding roundness of her breasts.

Her eyes were slumberous, unfocused, filled with something that he knew was only for him. Her lips were full and dewy, ripened by his desire, curved with pleasure. Her nipples were hard and beaded against his chest. He felt his own nipples tighten in response, beyond his control. It was a first for him. He was a man who directed his own fate, controlled what he took and bestowed.

She tightened her legs around his hips and curved against his erection, undulating while she caressed his hips and buttocks, moving her hands until she could cup him tightly.

He trembled and moaned, lifting his hips and thrusting his rigid shaft into her palm. He felt her fingers circle him, tightening and loosening her grasp with a slow, continual, excruciating pressure that had him gasping with each move of her hand. His erection expanded and grew in reaction, while the slim facade of control he'd had only moments ago slipped away from him.

"Maxie." He caught her wrist, and held her hand

still. "You keep that up and this'll be a replay of that episode in your room."

She stared up at him, eyes wide and dark in the early morning light. "I like to watch you come. You are so beautiful, Austin."

"How about I come inside you and you can watch me then," he said wryly, letting that "beautiful" comment rush over him like a seductive, hot wind. He loosened her fingers from around him, raised them to his mouth to graze the sensitive pads with his tongue and lips before kissing them, one by one.

"Okay. I'm easy." She smiled at him and he felt his chest constrict.

"Maxie, I can say with utmost certainly that you are not easy."

She thrust her lower lip out and said, "Are you saying I'm difficult, hard even?"

"Most definitely." His breath left in a rush as she cupped him again.

"I know hard, Austin. And I'm not anywhere near as hard as you. Your hardness makes me wet and needy."

His hand slipped down her body, sliding into the fold between her legs, seeing that she hadn't lied. She arched and cried out when he slid two fingers into her. "You are," he growled.

"Austin, please."

He shifted down onto his shoulder, wincing as the tattoo-tender skin ran alongside her back. "Please what?"

"Do what you want." She swallowed again, breath

catching, and shivered slightly, head dropping back against his shoulder. He let his hand drift farther up her side, farther up to tease the underside of her breast. "Whatever you want." She moaned when his fingers framed her breast, brushed lightly at her nipple. "I like that," she murmured. Another breath caught when he cupped and squeezed, dragged his hand down her belly to pull her buttocks tight against his loins. He drew her upper leg back across his hip, traced high up the inside of her thigh and rocked her against his erection. "Oh, Austin, that feels good."

"Good. It couldn't be anything else with you." His voice was a low murmur in her ear, sending his mouth on a hot, wayward tease along her neck. He hauled himself up to spoon tighter along her back, placed his thigh between hers and twisted a bit to zigzag a path of nipping kisses over her shoulder, down her side while his fingers loved and played, teased and tormented. He turned her upper body toward him.

"I know it—" With a slow, wicked movement, he dragged his tongue over her taut nipple. His lips curved around the bud with a wet slide, arching Maxie's back. She cried out when he drew hard. He could feel the hammering of her heart; her breathing altered and became harsh.

Austin lifted his head. "You like that?" He dropped his head and, his eyes riveted to her face while he took his time exploring her breast with his tongue, flirting with her nipple without touching it.

"Yes." She arched back, pleading, begging for respite. "Austin...Austin...please, I can't—"

She gasped and recoiled, thrusting her hips in un-controllable spasms when he curved his hand over her buttocks, slipped his hand between the slick center of her need and teased her with slow, measured circles. His arousal was hot and thick at the small of her back, her skin smooth and velvety.

She shifted her shoulders, took his face in her hands and took his mouth.

Darkness engulfed them, locked out everything but the intense energy that crackled around them, drawing them closer and closer together to join as one. Her restless hands molded over the long muscles of his thigh, her fingers kneading the hard curve of his but-tocks, until he couldn't stand any more of the excru-ciating pleasure.

He turned her onto her back and slipped between her thighs. She breathed deeply, her eyes half closed, watching him through the fringe of her lashes. She still felt dreamy, as if she was still asleep and he was a dream lover, yet she had never wanted so intensely as she did now, never hungered for a man as she did for him. The power of her need surprised her, because by nature she was a woman of great passion and verve, but he made her transcend that to some other amazing plane.

She came up off the bed, forcing him back so that his buttocks rested on his heels. Her breathing was ragged, her feelings intense, electrifying. She put her hands on his slick chest, letting the electric sensation seep into her skin with little prickles of heat. The touch of his skin was vital. She slipped her hands into his thick, dark hair, caressed with her thumb the silky hair at his hairline.

And for a long, heart-stopping moment she gazed into those sharp, intense eyes and saw something there that made her heart falter. Something she'd missed every time she'd looked at him. Something warm and sweet and so very tantalizing. The man he kept hidden. The man he wouldn't give to anyone, except now he was giving himself to her. A knife that cut two ways.

"Maxie, I..." His voice trailed off, filled with emotion, filled with need. Her fingers slid into his hair and she brought his mouth to hers. "It's all right, Austin. It's okay." His arms wrapped around her and he bore her back to the bed.

Her hand stroked down his back, curled around the hardness of his buttocks, moved around his magnificent body, her thumb caressed the blunt tip of his erection, spreading the result of his arousal around in smooth, exquisite circles. He growled deep in his throat and rolled, responding with an oath that sounded a lot like a prayer. His soft lips found hers and took them, drugging, no longer playful. The kiss coiled and corkscrewed through Maxie's blood with serpentine heat, ran roughshod over her senses. When he pulled her astride him, she settled there.

His hot brown eyes found her beautiful; his hands manipulated her hips, slid up her back forcing her to arch and thrust her breasts to his voracious mouth. She placed her hands on either side of his head and circled her hips while he suckled and laved her, stroking him, stoking him until they were both breathing harshly and mindless, rough with need.

"Maxie." Groaning, he searched the bed with his hand. "Where are they?"

"Huh?" Her body was on fire and she couldn't stop rocking, each exquisite motion making her separate father and father from sanity.

"Condoms. Please. I need...to protect..."

"Oh." Her thoughts were so disorganized from the excitement he gave to her, making her lose focus.

She climbed off him and looked over the side of the bed, fumbled along the edge of it until she came up with the box. Austin grabbed the box from her and pulled out a foil packet.

"Wait," she said.

He didn't answer, intent on getting the protection in place.

"Wait," she repeated and covered his hands with hers. "I want to do this." She pulled the bit of rubber out of its package and, eyes on his face, placed it over the tip of his arousal.

He made a low, deep sound of agreement and shoved hard into her hand. She unrolled the condom over his thickness. Then he hauled her underneath him.

He held her gaze, his big body pressing her into the mattress, and himself to the hilt with one thrust. Her body arched in feminine abandon at the force of his penetration, at this searing invasion. His penis was smooth and hard, thick, impossibly deep, and she writhed around him.

He steadied her, holding her firmly as he withdrew a little and thrust again, his gaze intent on her face. She couldn't stop her gasping cry at the intense, spiraling sensation, the pleasure that was almost agony. Her heart pounded fiercely against her ribs. She clung to him with desperate hands, feeling as if she were about to be torn apart by an internal force that was larger than she could hold. He whispered soothingly to her, words of masculine assurance she couldn't quite grasp, but the dark honey of his voice was more effective than any words.

"Please." She heard herself begging, for mercy, for relief, for anything and everything.

As if he understood her urgency even better than she, he pulled back and thrust deep, with a frantic hard need pushing him, kept it up until she convulsed around him and began to climax.

He rode her hard through the shuddering of her body. She had no control, no protection against the assault of intense feeling. He showed her no mercy as she went rigid like a strung bow. All she wanted was him, only him, the fierce intimacy of his body locked to hers.

For long moments she lay still, beneath him while her breathing slowed and the perspiration dried on her body. She was suddenly aware of Austin stroking her hair and wasn't sure how long he'd been doing that.

She closed her eyes tightly trying to hold onto her composure. It just wouldn't do to lose it now. She shifted her head and looked at the clock on the night table. Soon.

Too soon.

She kissed his chest, laving his nipples, sucking them into her mouth. Austin groaned raggedly, his hand clenching in her hair.

Too soon.

He began to harden inside her and Maxie groaned softly and moved against him.

If there was a frantic aspect in her lovemaking, Austin was matching it with his own, Maxie thought. It was as if he, too, was thinking this was the last time they would ever do this, the last time their hands would touch each other, caress each other and transcend the very confines of the flesh, closer than skin, closer than a whisper, closer than hearts.

He employed all that he had discovered about her body to propel her higher, harder. Maxie reciprocated loving the feel of every inch she touched, every gasp or groan. Her fingers sought out every curve of muscle, every hollow, until she could feel his heart throbbing beneath her fingertips.

She tangled her fingers in his hair, loving the silken feel of it against her oversensitive palms. She slid her hands over his shoulders, then down along the even, strong column of his back, one vertebra at a time. She cupped the satin smooth skin of his firm buttocks and urged him deeper into her. She nuzzled his chest, taking the masculine scent of him deep into her lungs. Kissing and flicking her tongue over his chest, she circled his taut nipples until they pulled even tighter and he let out a hissing breath.

He hastened the rhythm of his driving thrusts, and

Maxie welcomed the fierce pounding, crying out his name at the depth of each stroke, wishing it could go on forever and already crying inwardly because she knew it couldn't. She looked up at his face, curtained by the thick, dark strands of his hair. She reached up and pulled his head down toward her, driving her crazy with every movement of his slick body.

His gaze met hers then, and she saw the flash of understanding there. He shifted one hand to her blond hair and ran his hands through the short spikes. It was a moment of intense connection that touched something deep inside her, more intimate than the joining of their bodies, Maxie felt her heart heave and swell in response to the quiet physical dialogue.

She felt his hand slide between their bodies and knew it had touched him the same way, that moment of implicit unity. With a soft, anguished cry, her hips surged upward, begging for the touch that would send her over the edge. The pad of his finger gently probed until he found the nerve-rich center of her. With a guttural sound he caressed her, as his body maintained the excruciating, exhilarating tempo.

She pushed at him and rolled him over, sliding her hands up his arms, forcing his hands over his head close to the headboard. She reached over with a heavy heart and grabbed the cuffs and snapped them on, her fingers threading through his captured fingers.

And a moment later her body was gathering itself for a bittersweet release. She clutched at his shoulders, moaning. His nostrils flared, and he shifted himself slightly upward, his rigid flesh sliding over the spot he'd been stroking moments before he'd become manacled. She moaned, nearly screamed, as the convulsions took her, pulsing through her in hot, heavy beats, when his hard shaft entered her.

At the sound of a Harley outside, they both stiffened.

"Maxie?"

She tried to clear away the cramp in her throat, but a renewed sense of loss welled up in her and her vision blurred. How could she explain this to him so that he would understand? She couldn't bear what taking her in would do to him. More than she wanted to save her sister, she wanted to save Austin the agony. This was the only answer. She would take the decision out of his hands once and for all. For good. He wouldn't have to compromise his principles, his honor and duty would be intact and that gave her more satisfaction than any thing that she had ever done before in her life. Saving him made her whole.

The bed dipped as he shifted his weight, then he gasped as she shifted her hips. He was so close to orgasm the pleasure on his face so intense.

His eyes watched her with an unwavering stare, the dark stubble accentuating the stern set of his jaw. Compelled by the searching intensity of his eyes, she held his gaze, desolation nearly overwhelming her. Trying to clear her throat, she took a deep, unsteady breath, then forced herself to speak. "I've made such a mess of things," she whispered hoarsely. "I'm sorry."

11

"MAXIE," HE PROTESTED, pulling against the cuffs, but he was too far gone, the need for her overrode everything else.

She wanted to close her eyes. Anything more than what she was feeling right at this moment would be too much. But then Austin cried out her name, arching into her like a bow, throwing back his head as he thrust his hips against hers, and she couldn't look away from the beauty of his face as the pleasure took him. As the last spasms of her body died away, she felt the hot, molten rush as he pulsed inside her, shuddering under her as he said her name again in a low, guttural moan that was the sweetest sound she'd ever heard.

And the most mournful, for it was tinged with all the regret, all the acknowledgment of impossibility she herself was feeling.

And even though she knew nothing had changed, she couldn't regret having seen him like this one last time.

Austin was still breathing hard, his eyes closed when she moved off his body.

His eyes snapped open and he looked up at her with

such a sense of betrayal that Maxie almost gave up the whole plan, but then she thought of Dorrie and how she'd pledged her life savings to Maxie without a blink of an eye. How her sister had rallied to her side during the arrest. How her sister has always been there for her. She bit her lip, tears welling in her eyes. Maxie had to make it right.

"Don't do this, Maxie."

"I'm sorry, Austin," Maxie said, turning away from him. She quickly dressed and shoved all her stuff into her bag. "We've run out of time and it's the only way I can save you."

"Maxie, you don't have to save me. Please."

"I do because I...love you Austin. I know you probably don't believe that, but it's true." She turned back to him. "I have to go."

"If you love me, don't leave me like this, Maxie."

She walked around to the bed and searched through his jeans and finally found the key to the handcuffs in his boot. Tears spilled down her cheeks, hot and wet. Careful to keep her distance from him, she threw the blanket over his lower body. She walked to the door.

"It's the only way I can save you both. You'll see that later."

"The club really means that much to you?"

"No, you missed the point. Firecrackers is just glass, tables, chairs and liquor. What means something to me is the look in my sister's eyes. I can't disappoint her again." She put her hand on the door handle. "And turning me in will destroy you."

"Don't do this...Maxie."

"I think you know all about self-sacrifice, Austin. It's my turn now."

"Running away isn't going to solve anything. It'll only make matters worse. Let me take you back and we'll work everything out. Please give us a chance."

"I can't do that. There's too much at stake. Too much." She turned the knob, went out the door and pulled it closed. She could hear his ragged shout through the door.

"Maxie!"

"Are you all right, honey?" Star put her hand on her shoulder and Maxie turned around. With a sob of pure agony Maxie let Star enclose her in a hug.

"No, but it'll be okay."

"Isn't there any other way, honey?"

"No. I wish there were, but there isn't." She put the handcuff key in Star's hand. "Please let him go in a few hours."

"You're not going back to Mesa Roja, are you?"

"Not this time. But it wouldn't hurt if you could make him think I did."

"I'll try."

Maxie could see Handlebar waiting on his Harley not far from them. He waved to her and she waved back. "Star, there's something else I think you should know. Handlebar is in love with you. Why don't you give the big guy a break and go out with him?"

Star blushed and smiled. "Go out with him? I intend to marry the big oaf."

"Put him out of his misery, would you?"

Star nodded. "You call me when you get settled and if you ever need anything…" Star choked up and her lips tightened.

"I know. I'll call you." Maxie hugged Star and turned to the Harley, stowed her bag and started up the bike.

Just as suddenly, she turned the ignition to Off. As Star watched with a perplexed look on her face, Maxie walked over to Austin's car retrieved something from the rearview mirror, shoved it into her pocket and walked back to the bike. With a determined look on her face, she straddled the bike.

It rumbled to life again. This time, without a backward glance, she gunned the bike and as soon as she hit the pavement, she opened up the throttle. She hastily wiped the tears from her eyes. It wouldn't do to fog up her visor.

YOU EXPECTED THIS. You knew it was going to happen like this. So you have absolutely no right to be surprised.

Stepping out of the shower, Austin toweled himself off, rubbed at his hair. He walked into the bedroom, got dressed and went to the curtained window.

Star had come into the room an hour ago. Without a word she had unlocked the handcuffs and set him free.

When he had questioned her, she had tried to convince him that Maxie had gone back to Mesa Roja. But he knew in his heart that she hadn't. Maxie was gone.

Twenty minutes later, he grabbed a comb and began to drag it through his tangled hair, ordering himself to stop thinking about useless things he had no control over. Think about something you can do something about, he ordered himself.

He picked up his cell phone and dialed the number for Firecrackers.

"Firecrackers, Dorrie speaking."

"Ms. Maxwell. This is Austin Taggart."

"The bounty hunter." Maxie's sister's voice had gone flat.

"That's right."

"How is my sister?" Her concerned question only made him feel worse for what he was about to do.

"In deeper trouble," he replied with warning in his voice.

"Oh, no. How can she be in deeper trouble?"

"She escaped me this morning. "I need to find her. Where would she go?"

"Why should I tell you anything?"

"I don't have to report that she was aided and abetted by friends of hers." Austin didn't give a damn about the rough couple who had come here to help Maxie. He cared about finding her before she got into deeper trouble.

"Who?"

"Star Dupree and the biker she hangs out with."

She sighed. "Handlebar. She told me all about them. She loves them like family." There was a resignation in her voice.

"Do you want them to go to jail for your sister's reckless behavior?"

Dorrie let out a compressed breath. "No."

"Tell me where she is. Believe me, it'll be easier on her if I don't have to chase her down."

"You're putting me in an ugly place, Mr. Taggart." Dorrie's voice lowered and revealed her distress.

"No. Your sister put you there."

"You're compounding on it," she accused. And she had every right to accuse him. He was guilty, but he wasn't going to back down.

"All right, you win. Still doesn't get you off the hook," he said forcefully, trying to convince her that he meant business. "I'm going after your sister and I'll implicate her friends so that they, too, will go to jail. Your choice."

There was a pause and he deliberately kept quiet letting all he had said seep into her consciousness. He waited for her answer. "She probably went to a favorite B and B of hers. It's located in Colorado."

He released the breath he wasn't aware he was holding. "You're doing the right thing, Ms. Maxwell," he said as she gave him the name and directions to the B and B. "Thanks. I'll be in touch." He went to end the call, but her plea stopped him.

"Mr. Taggart. My sister means everything to me. Please don't hurt her."

"I have no intention—"

Dorrie Maxwell cut him off. "She's doing all this for me. Don't you think I understand that? But it doesn't matter. Not the club, not the money, not anything. If I could, I'd switch places with her. She's all that matters and I couldn't bear it if something happened to her because of me. Promise me you won't hurt her.''

''I'd never hurt her. I give you my promise.''

Long after his conversation with Dorrie Maxwell, Austin stood by the window, his eyes on the fading day, but he saw nothing. He'd been right about Maxie. She was trouble—major trouble.

He'd been kneed in the groin, led on a wild-goose chase and been betrayed. Now his heart was aching because he couldn't bear to destroy their dreams. He knew what that felt like and it hurt to think he would be responsible for taking away what they both wanted most—Firecrackers.

There were alternatives to taking her back. There had to be another angle.

The stars were just beginning to dot the sky with brilliance. *There's always another angle, son. All you have to do is look.*

His father's words came back to him on that star-studded night when he couldn't find Orion through his telescope.

Damn. Why hadn't he looked at it this way before? His heart felt lighter and more carefree.

He knew exactly what he was going to do.

He was going to let her go.

He loved her more than anything else on the planet. More than anything.

He turned to look at the bed and he could picture

her face. He wanted to run his hand over her shining hair. She was beautiful, inside and out.

He loved her. He knew it was true, but as with anything else in his life, he wasn't going to be able to keep her.

There was one more thing he could do for Maxie.

Tears pricked the back of his eyes as he closed them in order to gain the composure he would need. He walked to the door.

Closing it behind him, he went to the office to pay his bill. After that, there was nothing to do but get in his car. It wasn't until he was out of the parking lot that he realized that the small shield was gone from his rearview. He smiled softly. She didn't realize that now she wouldn't need it.

His cell phone rang and he automatically checked the number. When he recognized it as Manny's, he pushed the off button. Austin faced stoically forward and headed home to Sedona.

12

MAXIE WAS SO tired that she didn't think she could swing her leg over the bike and drag her tired body up the stairs of the B and B.

She was heartily sick of traveling and wanted nothing more than her comfortable apartment and her bed to sleep in. But the frilly, sweet-smelling room would have to do.

Of course, motels didn't bring back the memory of Austin. Of course, she could look at a tub and not think of how she'd pushed him into one. It was mind over matter after all. She wouldn't feel guilty.

She grabbed her bags and walked up the steps, signed in as quickly as possible and went up to her room. It didn't take long to run a bath and drop in soothing bath salts. She sank into the hot water with a soft sigh.

He must hate her for the humiliating way she had left him. She would never forget the look on his face, the pain in his eyes. It would haunt her for a very long time. Even if she wanted to go back to Sedona and turn herself in, he would never forgive her.

Not that she was thinking about turning herself in. She couldn't turn herself in.

After the water cooled, she toweled off and dressed in one of Austin's T-shirts she'd accidentally stuffed in her bag three days ago. Three days since she'd cuffed him to that bed in the hotel where she'd finally admitted to herself that she was in love with him. She wondered if Austin had followed her.

She lay down on the bed and leaned back against the pile of pillows. She held the shield up, staring at it, outlined each bold line of paint with her finger, amazed at the skill it took to draw on such a small canvas.

She'd like to see the old woman at work.

She yearned to see Austin again and have him pull her into his strong arms.

"Running away isn't going to solve your problems."

Austin's warning echoed in her head, in her heart. Eventually she slept, but sporadically, her light sleep made restive by guilty dreams that woke her up with a vague feeling of uneasiness. It was a twisting, winding sort of sleep, fractured and chaotic. When the first light of dawn began to streak across the sky she felt more tired than when she had first lain down.

She looked once more at the small shield she'd held through the night. Perhaps it could bring her luck when she went back to Sedona, as she knew she must.

Austin was right. She had to face her problems and stop running from them. She tried his cell phone number one more time, but there was still no answer.

She wondered if he'd shut it off to keep her from calling. She disconnected the call and left no message.

Deciding not to call her sister because Maxie didn't want her to worry, she dressed, paid her bill and straddled the bike. If she rode hard, she could be back in Sedona in four days. Back to face the music. Back to face the embezzlement charges and hope that Jake had something she could use.

She wondered if Austin would be proud of her. She wondered if he would ever know or care.

ALMOST SIX WEEKS after she had left Sedona, she was now back, and walking into the very place where she had been booked. Sedona's Seventh precinct raged with pandemonium. It seemed that the cops had just busted a group of hookers in a raid and there were women yelling and kicking cops all over the lobby.

Maxie stepped around an especially tall woman and peered up at the desk sergeant.

"Excuse me."

"I don't want to hear your sob story. Tell it to the judge." The words were so similar to Austin's that Maxie's heart contracted.

Maxie stared up at him, her throat tight. "I don't have a story. I just came to…"

"Martinez, will you get over here and get this pesky woman into a cell," the desk sergeant bellowed.

A burly officer grabbed her arm, but Maxie fought him. "Look, I'm a fugitive from justice and I do belong in a cell, but not for solicitation."

The desk sergeant studied her features. "I know who you are. Francesca Maxwell."

"That's right." She turned to the officer and said, "Now you can take me to a cell."

"Hold up there, Martinez. She's not going to any cell."

Maxie gave the man a perplexed look. The fear in her subsided and was replaced by hope.

The desk sergeant's whole demeanor changed and he smiled at her. "Welcome back, little lady. It seems we owe you an apology."

"What do you mean? I've come to turn myself in."

"No need. You're free to go."

"I am?"

"A Jake Utah came down to the precinct with evidence that your associate at the bank, Mark Irvin, planned and executed the whole embezzlement scheme. When he was hauled in and we presented the evidence, he said that he used your code and framed you. The local authorities and the FBI have dropped the charges and plan to give you a formal apology."

Stunned, elated, Maxie stared at the desk sergeant for a moment then she spoke, "Jake's come through for me."

"Yes, he did."

"What about the flight charges?"

"Those have been dropped, too. We're not about to haul an innocent victim into court and press charges for flight and cost the taxpayers an expensive trial."

Maxie had to sit down. She did so in the midst of the bustling precinct across from the wanted posters on the wall. She was completely relieved. Evidently

Jake had gotten her off the hook. She owed Jake everything.

"JAKE, I INSIST on paying for the computer hacker you used to help me." Maxie had left the station and immediately gone over to Jake's home. She'd found him setting up a new, state-of-the-art computer. Now, she was in a full debate with him over the money she felt she owed him.

"Maxie, don't worry about it. I've already been compensated for my part in this because I was instrumental in finding the lost money. I should share it with you." He attached cords and wires. "I'm glad it's all over. You—" he looked at her "—a fugitive from justice. Hard to believe. I thank God that nothing terrible happened to you when you were running from the law."

He put down the equipment and hugged her close in a brotherly embrace. Then he let her go and sat down in front of the screen.

"Jake, I'm so grateful, please let me do this, at least."

"No." He keyed in the software code and manipulated the mouse.

"I want to pay you."

He shrugged his broad shoulders. "Maxie, will you drop it?"

"No, I won't." She searched around on his desk. "Where's the invoice or agreement? Tell me the amount."

"You said you would introduce me to your sister.

That's all I want. With the reward money I'm going to invest in your club.''

Maxie threw up her hands, feeling anxiety for the first time in her life. ''It seems that I owe someone, somehow. Fine, Jake. Who was the hacker? I'll call him myself and ask him.''

''No. You can't do that.''

''Why?''

''I wasn't supposed to tell where I got the money to pay Mike. He made me promise.''

Maxie drew back and looked at him with surprise. ''Who made you promise?''

Jake looked away from her. ''Big Native American guy named Austin.''

''Austin?''

''Yeah, he's intimidating. Not the type to take no for an answer. I liked him, though. I told him I'd reimburse him the moment I got the reward money, but he refused.'' But when Jake turned back to look at her, he realized he was talking to thin air. Maxie was gone.

MAXIE TRIED AUSTIN'S cell phone as soon as she got into her car. And finally it was picked up. Her heart beat nervously against the wall of her chest.

''Hello?'' The voice was soft and definitely female. Maxie almost hung up, but that wouldn't help her. If Austin already had another girlfriend, then she'd have to be content to thank him and let that be the end of it.

''Who is this?''

"Jessica."

Relief washed through Maxie. "You probably don't know me, but I've heard a lot about you."

"You have?"

"Yes, I'm the most recent bounty he didn't collect on."

"Blondie." Jessica squealed.

"What?"

"That's what he called you. It's really amazing what he did for you. I can't believe he sold his car, but that's just the way he is."

"Sold his car?" Maxie felt her insides clench.

"Sure."

"Oh, please, no. Not that. Do you know who he sold it to?"

"I sure do."

Maxie wrote down the information as Jessica told her.

"Could I talk to him?"

"He's out with a friend looking for a new car."

"Do me a favor and please don't tell him I called." Jessica agreed and Maxie never looked back.

13

IF SHE HAD KNOWN that the Mustang handled this well, she'd have made Austin let her drive it. She parked in front of the well-kept two-story house, picked up the large bouquet of columbine tied with a red ribbon and got out. Walking up to the front porch, she knocked on the door. A beautiful eighteen-year-old woman eventually opened it.

"Jessica?"

"Maxie?"

They hugged as if they'd known one another all their lives. "I'm sure glad you came." When she spied the car in the driveway a grin spilt her face. "Oh, that's a good bribe."

"Austin doesn't take bribes. This is a gift."

Jessica laughed. "Okay. It's a good gift. What are those?"

"Columbine. Austin said the seeds were used to cure headaches. I think I gave him a pretty big one when I ran him around in circles. I thought maybe his grandmother would know how to brew a remedy."

Jessica laughed. "You are pretty funny, Maxie. Why don't you come through the house? His place is out back.'' The house was beautiful, furnished in tasteful southwestern chic with colorful Apache blankets and pottery.

When they reached the patio, Maxie saw the small, neat house that sat twenty-five feet away from the main house.

''Austin had it built when my grandmother moved in. He said we needed our privacy.'' Jessica rolled her eyes. ''It's my guess he's the one who needed his privacy.''

Maxie opened the sliding glass door, went out across the patio until she got to his front door. She knocked and waited. Finally, the door opened and Austin stood in the doorway. He didn't say anything he just stood there.

''I found out what you did.''

''I don't want to be repaid.'' He closed the door in her face.

His mistake was, he didn't lock it. She wasn't sure even that would have kept her out.

She went in and made a flying leap for his back. The flowers broke from the bundle and rained down on them. When she landed on him, it pushed him forward right into a bunch of pillows he kept in front of a beautiful kiva fireplace.

When he got himself turned around, Maxie straddled his lap. ''You're going to listen to me. I have something to say.''

''You always have something to say—you never shut up.''

''That's right, so let me say what I came here to

say because the last time I said it, it wasn't very romantic.... I love you.''

There was a sudden glimmer of raw emotion in his eyes, and he abruptly looked away. Maxie saw him try to swallow. He waited a moment then looked back at her. "Are you sure I'm the right man for you?"

"You didn't come after me when you had the chance. Dorrie told me everything. You knew where I was, but you let me go. You sold your car. You refused to be reimbursed for the money you laid out to that hacker of Jake's. I know you're the right man for me. You don't care that I like bikers and llamas. That I would rather go dirt biking then do the laundry. I'm spontaneous and you're not. So you can balance me out and I'll balance you out.''

She held her breath when Austin didn't reply. His face was still, his eyes dark and fathomless. God, she could get lost in those eyes forever—free fall into soft honey velvet. With a rough outburst of air, he clenched his eyes shut and hauled her into his arms. "I love everything about you, blondie.'' Tightening his grasp, he whispered against her hair, his voice ragged. "I need you in my life, someone who knows how to surprise me.''

Maxie wound her arms around his neck, squeezing her eyes closed with relief that she hadn't lost Austin. "Good. We can start with what's in the driveway.'' She raised her eyebrows up and down. "You were right about everything. I had to come back. It was the right thing to do.'' She got off him and helped him up. "The way I left you...I felt so bad that I couldn't stand it anymore. I'm sorry."

"Don't be. You did what you thought you had to do." He paused then asked, "What about the club?"

"The license came four days ago. The club's fine, especially now that you cleared my name."

He looked away from her. "I figured that it was something I could do for you."

"You make me feel grounded, Austin. It's not something I'm accustomed to."

His eyes narrowed a fraction, and he stared at her, his gaze suddenly dark and serious. "Get accustomed to it, blondie. I'm crazy in love with you." He stared at her for an instant longer, then he closed his eyes and pressed into her, his unchecked strength nearly crushing her. There was silence for some time as he just held on to her, as if he couldn't let her go, and Maxie closed her eyes and clung to him.

"What's with the flowers? A peace offering?"

"You said they cured headaches and I thought it couldn't hurt to bring them. Maybe your grandmother could figure out how to make the remedy."

He threw back his head and laughed, holding her tight.

"Come on, Austin. Come see what I got you."

"I'm afraid to look," he said huskily, following her out the door and around the house. When they turned the corner, Austin stopped dead and stared.

He stared at the car so long that Maxie wondered if he had turned to stone.

He looked at her, the muscles in his jaw bunched. He inhaled roughly. "That's my car," he said softly.

"Yes. It's your car."

He turned to her. "How could you afford to buy my car back?"

"Jake bought me out. I divested in Firecrackers."

"No, Maxie. I won't let you do that."

"Wait. I haven't told you everything. Jake gave me some of the reward money. After I bought the car back, I reinvested almost all the money. You'll never guess where."

"Where?"

"The Lucky Star. I want to go back to Mesa Roja and live. I loved it there."

He laughed, gathered her up in his arms and whirled her around. "You are one spontaneous woman."

She looked up into his eyes and smiled. "Yes I am and I'm one lucky woman now that I have you, Austin."

"So what are you going to do with the money you saved?"

"What?"

"You said you reinvested almost all of the money."

"Well, I didn't actually save it. Look in the back seat of the car."

He walked over to the back seat and she saw him swallow hard and brace himself against the window.

She walked up to him and saw that he was overcome with emotion. "I don't know if it's like the one your father bought you, but the clerk at the electronics store said it was powerful. I want to touch the stars with you.''

He buried his face in her neck and gathered her close to him. Maxie closed her eyes and was glad that she could give him something that had so much meaning.

''I didn't expect you to come back. I thought I'd lost you.''

''No way. You could never lose me.'' She pressed her hand to his heart. ''Keep me right here for the rest of my life.''

He kissed her and it was the cheering from the upstairs window that drew them apart.

She smiled up into his face. ''That would be your family.''

''Yes, it would. Why don't you come in and meet them?''

And Maxie did with her heart full and her step light.

Epilogue

"Mrs. Granger, you shouldn't eat all the gumdrops in one sitting," Maxie scolded as they rocked out in front of the Taggarts' main house. "Austin will be here any minute to drive us to Handlebar... I mean David and Star's wedding. You won't have any room for cake."

"What do I have to worry about? My health? Dear, I can eat as much candy and cake as I want, if you haven't noticed—I'm old."

"Then you should stop acting like a child." Maxie smiled, but took the gumdrops out of Mrs. Granger's hands.

"Oh my, the roller coaster sure looks fine in that uniform," Mrs. Granger said with an appreciative tone in her voice.

Maxie looked out toward the driveway as Austin walked around his cruiser. The tan sheriff's uniform looked very, very good on him. His eyes were hidden behind a pair of mirrored sunglasses and a tan Stetson covered his shiny black hair, although nothing could stop the impact of this hot, dangerous man.

"Star's sure glad that you decided to buy an interest in her roadhouse. Why, your ideas have transformed that place."

Austin came onto the porch.

"Hi, handsome. If you're looking for some criminals, you've come to the wrong place," Maxie teased.

"I don't know about that, blondie. It's sure criminal for you ladies to be so beautiful." He smiled and leaned down to give his wife a kiss.

Mrs. Granger got up from her rocker. "I'll go get my wrap and let your grandmother, mother and sister know you're here."

Maxie looked up at him. "You look good enough to eat, Austin."

"Mmm. We have a wedding to attend. There's no time for any naughtiness," he said, censure in his eyes.

"That's too bad. I can think of so many different ways to be bad." She gave him a look full of sin.

"Don't make me arrest you. I have handcuffs," he threatened softly, his eyes telling her that he'd love it right now if she were bad.

"Don't tempt me, Austin," Maxie said softly as she got up and wrapped her arms around her husband's waist.

Austin laughed as he felt her try to lift the cuffs. "Oh, no, you don't. The last time we had to call the fire department when you accidentally kicked the key down the grate."

"Okay, I'll wait until tonight, if I have to." Maxie backed into her chair and caught her hose. It ripped un in the nylon. "Will you look at that? Now I have to change."

"Looks like you'll need my assistance ma'am." Austin pulled the radio from his belt and spoke into it while a slow smile spread across her face. "We'll still have plenty of time to get you to the church." For a moment, Austin crushed her to him, so tightly in his arms that only the two of them existed.

"Get a room," Jessica groused as she walked around them and down to the cruiser that had just pulled up. "You better hurry up, Maxie."

"Just have to change my hose," Maxie said with a grin. "Do you have any spare?"

"Yes, I do. In my top dresser drawer," Jessica said.

Mrs. Granger and Austin's mother and grandmother approached them. "I can see the sun will burn a long time for you," his grandmother whispered to Austin.

He smiled down at Maxie. "Yes, grandmother, I believe that it will."

Maxie watched as her family got into the cruiser and drove off. She deftly grabbed the cuffs at Austin's belt.

Austin smiled as he followed her into the house.

The Trueblood, Texas
tradition continues in...

TRULY, MADLY, DEEPLY
by Vicki Lewis Thompson
August 2002

Ten years ago Dustin Ramsey and Erica Mann shared their first
sexual experience. It was a disaster. Now Dustin's determined
to find—and seduce—Erica again, determined to prove to
her, and himself, that he can do better. Much, *much* better.
Only, little does he guess that Erica's got the same agenda....

*Don't miss Blaze's next two sizzling Trueblood tales,
written by fan favorites Tori Carrington and Debbi Rawlins.
Available at your nearest bookstore
in September and October 2002.*

Princes...Princesses...
London Castles...New York Mansions...
To live the life of a royal!

In 2002, Harlequin Books lets you escape to a world of royalty with these royally themed titles:

Temptation:
January 2002—*A Prince of a Guy* (#861)
February 2002—*A Noble Pursuit* (#865)

American Romance:
The Carradignes: American Royalty (Editorially linked series)
March 2002—*The Improperly Pregnant Princess* (#913)
April 2002—*The Unlawfully Wedded Princess* (#917)
May 2002—*The Simply Scandalous Princess* (#921)
November 2002—*The Inconveniently Engaged Prince* (#945)

Intrigue:
The Carradignes: A Royal Mystery (Editorially linked series)
June 2002—*The Duke's Covert Mission* (#666)

Chicago Confidential
September 2002—*Prince Under Cover* (#678)

The Crown Affair
October 2002—*Royal Target* (#682)
November 2002—*Royal Ransom* (#686)
December 2002—*Royal Pursuit* (#690)

Harlequin Romance:
June 2002—*His Majesty's Marriage* (#3703)
July 2002—*The Prince's Proposal* (#3709)

Harlequin Presents:
August 2002—*Society Weddings* (#2268)
September 2002—*The Prince's Pleasure* (#2274)

Duets:
September 2002—*Once Upon a Tiara/Henry Ever After* (#83)
October 2002—*Natalia's Story/Andrea's Story* (#85)

**Celebrate a year of royalty with
Harlequin Books!**

Available at your favorite retail outlet.

HARLEQUIN®
Makes any time special®

Visit us at www.eHarlequin.com

HSROY02

eHARLEQUIN.com

community | membership

buy books | authors | online reads | magazine | learn to write

buy books

♥ We have your favorite books from Harlequin, Silhouette, MIRA and Steeple Hill, plus bestselling authors in Other Romances. Discover savings, find new releases and fall in love with past classics all over again!

online reads

♥ Read daily and weekly chapters from Internet-exclusive serials, and decide what should happen next in great interactive stories!

magazine

♥ Learn how to spice up your love life, play fun games and quizzes, read about celebrities, travel, beauty and so much more.

authors

♥ Select from over 300 Harlequin author profiles and read interviews with your favorite bestselling authors!

community

♥ Share your passion for love, life and romance novels in our online message boards!

learn to write

♥ All the tips and tools you need to craft the perfect novel, including our special romance novel critique service.

membership

♥ FREE! Be the first to hear about all your favorite themes, authors and series and be part of exciting contests, exclusive promotions, special deals and online events.

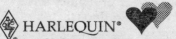

HARLEQUIN®

Makes any time special®—online...

Visit us at
www.eHarlequin.com

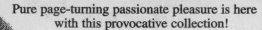

HARLEQUIN®
Temptation.

Look for bed, breakfast and more...!

COOPER'S CORNER

Some of your favorite Temptation authors are checking in early at Cooper's Corner Bed and Breakfast

In May 2002:

**#877 *The Baby and the Bachelor*
Kristine Rolofson**

In June 2002:

**#881 *Double Exposure*
Vicki Lewis Thompson**

In July 2002:

**#885 *For the Love of Nick*
Jill Shalvis**

In August 2002 things heat up even more at Cooper's Corner. There's a whole year of intrigue and excitement to come—twelve fabulous books bound to capture your heart and mind!

**Join all your favorite Harlequin authors
in Cooper's Corner!**

HARLEQUIN®
Makes any time special®

HTCC